FATE + CHANCE = LOVE

(THE BLAKE FAMILY SERIES)

R.C. STERN

Cover Design by StunningBookCovers.com
Formatting by Polgarus Studio

ISBN-13: 978-0-9965278-0-4 (Kindle)
ISBN-13: 978-0-9965278-1-1 (epub)
ISBN-13: 978-0-9965278-2-8 (print)

To my amazing husband and our wonderful boys…
you guys are forever my world.
Semper Ad Meliora

CHAPTER ONE

May – one year earlier

CARI

"Look at all the man candy waiting to get in!" My best friend Rodrigo shouts as he checks out all the eye candy standing in line outside of the club. We're celebrating my birthday with Rodrigo's brother, German, at Club XTC - the hottest, glitziest, and most prestigious three level club in Manhattan. It is *the* club to be seen in, and the club celebrities are known to visit frequently.

The swank club has two separate entrances. The covered entrance graced with the red carpet on the left is for VIP's only. Inside the building there is a separate floor exclusively for this elite crowd. The entrance on the right is for the general public, and there's always a line to get in. Fortunately for us, Rodrigo and I have been placed on the VIP list courtesy of German who is chatting with the bouncer when we arrive. German gives his brother a fist bump, and then gives me a kiss on the cheek and a bear hug. The bouncer wishes me a happy birthday and waves us in.

A hostess greets us inside and leads us to an elevator. We ride the glass elevator to the second level where we get off and step onto the polished marble floor. Rodrigo and I simultaneously drop our mouths as we take in the scene.

At the far end of the room is the bar which spans almost the entire length of that one side. It's crowded and there are four bartenders each busy making drinks. One of them does a fancy move with the shaker like Tom

Cruise did in *Cocktails*. The hostess shows us to our reserved booth, and we thank her. German whispers something to her and she giggles. He's such a big flirt. I notice the crowded dance floor which is a half level down.

"I've never been to such a fancy club," I say.

"This is the best in New York. Everyone wants to be here," German says.

"Did you sleep with the hostess to get us VIP passes?" Rodrigo asks.

"Now Rodrigo you know a gentleman doesn't tell his secrets," German says and chuckles leaving us to wonder if he really did shack up with the hostess.

The waitresses are outfitted in a black lace up bustier with a very short black skirt, and the waiters are in tight black t-shirts and black slacks. Rodrigo is salivating over the hot men. Our waitress introduces herself to us and takes our orders. German orders us a round of tequila shots to start, and then tells us to order whatever we want as he is picking up the tab.

I order a cosmopolitan, and Rodrigo gives her his order. I arch an eyebrow at him. "Horny bull?"

"Feeling it tonight." He wiggles his eyebrows making German laugh while I shake my head.

"Are there any celebrities here tonight?" I ask German.

"Of course, but they are usually on the third level for privacy reasons. They're VVIP's, and rarely hang on this level. We're just VIP's."

"We're still important."

"We are. Just not *that* important."

Rodrigo looks around fanning himself. "There's so much man candy here tonight. I bet there is bound to be one guy – "

I wave my hands and cut him off. "Rodrigo, I am not in the market for a boyfriend." My love life has been nonexistent for a few years now. My last relationship left me scarred so badly that I am hesitant to hit the dating scene again.

"I'm not talking about for you honey. I meant for me." As this is not a gay club it would be very slim pickings for Rodrigo.

"Oh." My cheeks flush from the mistake.

German laughs. "You know Cari I think it wouldn't hurt for you to look too." I roll my eyes at his comment.

"It's time to move on," Rodrigo says.

I do want to move on. If only it were that easy to move on. I let out a deep sigh. "I know you're both right, but every time I think –"

Rodrigo puts his hand up to stop me. "Forget about Evil."

"Everett," I correct him.

Rodrigo never could get his name right. He has no love for the guy who wrecked me. He sighs. "Evil, Everett...what's the difference? He's still a douchebag, and deserves to have his nuts toasted to a crisp. If you don't try to move on you never will."

"I gotta agree with my brother. Cari, you're young and gorgeous." German's comment makes me blush. "And most of all you deserve to be happy."

I do not like being reminded of my ex-boyfriend who I dated during my freshman year in college. He ruined what should have been an exciting first year for me, and it took months of therapy before I finally started to recover. The therapist encouraged me to resume dating. I want to start dating again, and allow myself a chance at happiness again. If only I can let go of my fear of being hurt.

Our waitress returns to the table with our drinks.

Rodrigo raises his shot glass. "Happy birthday my dear Cari. May all your dreams and wishes come true, and may you find yourself a hottie tonight."

"Happy birthday sweetheart!" German joins in. We clink our shot glasses. "And let's also toast to your final year in college."

Here goes. We down our shots at the same time. Whoa! My throat burns as the alcohol passes through, but it feels great.

"You two excited to start your senior year?"

"Hell yeah!" Rodrigo says. "I can't wait to be done with school and start making money so I don't have to work with dad." We all laugh because their father wants his children to go into orthodontics to help him with his practice, but Rodrigo wants no part of it. His dream job does not entail teeth.

"Enjoy each day and you too darling." German winks at me.

"I will. I wish Grams and Gramps were still around." I couldn't hide the sadness in my voice. I missed my grandparents.

Rodrigo takes my hand and gives it a squeeze. "Don't be sad. We're all so very proud of you Cari, and we'll always be your family."

"I'm not going to be sad. We're here to celebrate. And thank you German for making it possible to celebrate my birthday here."

"You got it. Listen kids, I'm going to go dance. Come out when you're ready."

"I came out a long time ago."

I let out a giggle. German slaps Rodrigo on the back of his head. On his way to the dance floor, he is stopped by a blonde who ends up accompanying him. Rodrigo and I people watch as we leisurely finish our drinks. After taking the last swallow of our drinks, Rodrigo grabs my hand and leads me onto the dance floor.

We dance to a couple of songs when I catch a cute guy eyeing Rodrigo. Uh-oh. It's only a matter of minutes before he eyes him back. The DJ pumps up the music, and the guy who has been watching Rodrigo approaches him and they start talking. I'm hoping Rodrigo will not abandon me, but he does. He mouths an apology to me and shimmies away with the cute guy. *Great.* I start to make my way back to our booth when a tall, blonde guy stops me.

"Hi there. Name's Donovan."

"Hi."

"First time here?"

I nod. He smiles at me, but something about his smile makes me nervous. He takes another step closer to me, and I can smell the alcohol in his breath along with his unpleasant body odor. *Ewww!*

"Let me buy you a drink beautiful."

I shift to my left to put some distance between us. "Thank you, but perhaps another time." I spin around and push my way through the crowded dance floor. I don't get too far when his arm wraps around my waist pulling me back against his chest. Can't Donovan take a hint? I break free from his grasp and turn around ready to slap him, but my hand becomes suspended in mid-air. I let out a gasp, and he takes a step back. *He's not Donovan.*

The guy standing before me is the most attractive male specimen I have ever laid eyes on. He's tall, and devastatingly handsome. His hair is neatly pulled back into a man ponytail. The blue dress shirt he is wearing hugs his broad muscular shoulders, and the top buttons of his shirt are undone exposing a chain hanging from his neck. He is very hot. No, scratch that. He is very, very hot. And he is making me feel hot. The intensity of his gaze is about to burn a hole right through me. For the first time in years my heart starts to pound hard.

"Was that guy bothering you?" His voice is deep, smooth, and sexy making me forget who he is asking about. He sees the confusion on my face so he motions with his head to show me who he is referring to. Donovan. I shake my head. He leans in and I get a whiff of his cologne. He smells so good.

"Dance with me."

Me? He could have his pick of any of the beautiful women here tonight, but he wants *me* to dance with him. Speechless, I offer a nod as acceptance. He starts to move his hips and I move with him. There's an inexplicable force drawing me to him. I find it impossible to look away from his heated gaze. We are so close my breasts and his chest briefly meet sending jolts of electricity through my body. He slowly slides his arm around my waist, and I practically melt from the contact.

"What's your name?"

"Cari…spelled C-a-r-i." *Oh my God.* Did I really just spell my name for him? Clearly the alcohol is getting to me.

"Cari. It's a beautiful name for a beautiful lady." My cheeks heat from his compliment.

We are no longer dancing to the beat of the music, but instead dancing to our own beat. He reaches out and tucks a piece of loose hair behind my ear. My eyes focus on his lips. *Lips I want to taste.* As if he has the ability to read my mind, he leans his face closer to mine, and I can feel his warm breath on my face. My heart is racing. He presses his lips to mine, and I close my eyes. His lips are warm, and soft. The kiss is light, and gentle.

"What the fuck?"

Startled, we both pull apart. A vehement blonde stares at us with daggers in her eyes. *Oh God.* She must be his girlfriend. What was I thinking kissing a stranger? Embarrassed and disappointed, I mutter an apology and quickly make my escape before she pounces on me. I nearly trip over my own feet rushing back to the table. I am surprised to find Rodrigo sitting there sipping away at another drink.

"There you are sweetie!"

"Come on. We need to go."

"Go? Like leave?" I nod. "We haven't even been here that long!"

I plead with him. "Yes. Now. Please."

Looking down to the dance floor, I catch him staring up at me. He frowns while his girlfriend grinds her body against his. I look away and drag Rodrigo out of the club. We head to the nearest subway station and take a train back to German's apartment. Rodrigo sends a text to his brother letting him know we left.

"Why in the world were you rushing me out of the club?"

"I didn't want to stay."

The look on his face tells me he's not buying my reason. The subway rolls into the station, and we get on. I stare up at the advertisements in the subway car.

"Something happened. Am I going to have to drag it out of you?" My best friend knows me too well. "Oh shit. Did you run into douchebag?"

"No."

"Then what is it sweetie? What had you running out of there?"

"I was dancing with this guy when his girlfriend showed up."

Rodrigo claps his hand over his heart and gasps loudly earning looks from the other passengers. "You danced with a stranger?"

"Can you please keep it down?"

"Sorry, sorry, sorry. You just took me by surprise."

"You abandoned me on the dance floor, and then some guy hit on me. I walked away and this other guy was there."

"So who was he? Was he hot?"

"Yeah. He was very hot."

"How did I miss him? What happened when the girlfriend showed up?"

There's no way I'm going to share with him the tiny detail of the kiss. "She wasn't happy. It was embarrassing. I didn't know he had a girlfriend so I left him with her."

"If my boyfriend was that hot I would not let him out of my sight."

"A hot guy like that is nothing but trouble."

He pats my hand. "They usually are. Don't worry honey, there's more fish under the sea."

My eyebrows furrow. "Actually, it's more fish *in* the sea."

"That's what I said."

I shake my head and laugh.

Yes, there may be more fish in the sea, but there was something about that one fish. Something more.

CHAPTER TWO

DEVEN

It's been a couple of weeks since Bradley and I last came to Club XTC. I had no plans on coming here tonight, but Brad was persistent we come here before our trip to Los Angeles on Monday.

Brad is like a brother to me. Paired as roommates in our freshman year at the University of Pennsylvania, we immediately hit it off. We shared a lot of common ground - music, cars, and political views to name a few. The both of us even made it into the same fraternity. Brad grew up in Boston, and has that unique Boston accent which I first thought sounded strange coming from an Asian-American. Regardless of his accent, he is very intelligent, ambitious, and dedicated to his job at BG.

When it comes to relationships, that's where Brad and I differ. He's always been a player. He's not ready to settle down anytime soon. I want a serious relationship with the girl that's perfect for me. Someone that's not only beautiful, but also intelligent. Someone I can connect with. Someone I can love, cherish, protect, trust, and make mine completely.

We are seated at our regular table. Not too soon after we order our drinks, a couple of girls approach our table. I remember them from the last time we were here. The blonde is Angie, and the redhead is Delila. They're nice-looking girls, but shallow. Shallow, mindless girls do not interest me. Their flirting turns me off, but Brad seems to enjoy it. They invite us to dance with them. Brad's face lights up with a smile. Yup, he's definitely looking to get lucky tonight. He's such a manwhore. I'm certainly not in the mood to dance with either of them so I choose to stay behind.

The ladies in the next table attempt to flirt with me, but I ignore them.

I turn my attention to the dance floor, and my eyes stumble upon a stunning brunette. I do a double take. *Jesus Christ*. She's laughing away as she dances with a guy who seems to delight in shaking his ass a little too much.

Who is she? I'm mesmerized by her beauty. Her long straight hair falls just past her shoulders, and the tight, short sexy dress she has on shows off her gorgeous figure, and lovely long legs.

"Christ almighty! Who is that babe?" Brad asks.

I'll be damned if he is going to hit on her before I do. "Back so soon? What happened? Girls ditched you?"

"They started to dance with a group of their girlfriends. Thought I'd admire them instead," Brad says and takes a swig of his drink.

I turn back around to watch *her* again.

"How the hell did I not see her when I was out there?"

I give him a warning look. "Forget it. I laid eyes on her first."

He slaps me on the back. "Glad you're still interested in chicks. I thought you were swearing off women."

I let out a laugh. "No, not at all. She's with someone though."

"Nope."

I give him a questioning look.

"That guy she's with is gay."

"And how would you know?"

"I have a gay cousin. I can spot them a mile away," I laugh because it's true. "Are you going to go talk to her?"

"Yes. I think I am."

"I'm going to ask one of those girls at the next table if they want to dance. Maybe I'll score tonight." I've never known him to stick with just one girl. It's remarkable he hasn't contracted one fucking STD yet.

Brad makes his move at the table full of girls while I make my way to the dance floor in my quest to speak to that beautiful girl. I weave through the dancing crowd to catch up to the beautiful brunette, but some guy stops her first. The exchange between them is brief, but I can see from the look on her face she is terrified. I go to rescue her from him, but she walks away from the creep turning every guy's head as she does. I follow her determined not to let her out of my sight.

I manage to catch up to her and wrap one arm around her waist pulling her back to me. Damn, she smells heavenly…like vanilla and almond. Her body stiffens. She frees herself from my grip and whirls around. Fuck me. *She's gorgeous.* I've never seen anyone as beautiful as she is. I feel weak at the knees. Since when do I get weak at the knees over a woman? I notice she's about to slap me so I step back, but her hand never connects to my face. She drops her hand and I ask her if that asshole was harassing her. She shakes her head.

I ask her to dance with me, and she gives me a nod. I put my arm around her waist again and draw her close to me. I ask her for her name, and she tells me it's Cari. It's beautiful just like her and I tell her so.

The attraction between us is undeniable. I gently sweep her hair behind her ears and let my fingers slightly graze her soft skin. So beautiful. I'm not one for PDA's, but there's something about her. I can't stop myself from dipping my head to kiss her. She tastes so fucking sweet…like candy. Her lips are soft and delicious, and –

"What the fuck?"

We tear apart. I look over and it's the damn leech Angie. Why can't she leave me the fuck alone? Before I even have a chance to tell Angie to go, Cari whispers something softly and rushes off.

I want to go after her, but Angie grabs hold of my arm and halts me. My eyes scan the dance floor for Cari in the sea of people, but I don't see her. Then something from the upper level catches my eye. It's Cari. She's staring right back as Angie grinds against me. Angie's had a little too much to drink. I try to excuse myself, but she doesn't let go of me, and it's rather annoying. I decide to be honest and tell her I'm not interested in her. Well, that did it. She tells me to fuck off, and I do. I hurry back upstairs to look for Cari, but she's nowhere in sight.

Desperate, I locate Sasha to assist me. She's the manager of the club and is ten years older than I am, but still attractive. She has a crush on me, but the feeling is not mutual. I consider her to be a friend only, and I think she's finally starting to accept that. Sasha smiles widely when she sees me. I ask her to help me find Cari. I describe Cari to her, and she leads me to the surveillance room introducing me to the security manager. He replays some of the video and I look at the footage only to see that I am too late. She already left the club.

CHAPTER THREE

May - one year later

CARI

"Is my toiletry case in that box?" Rodrigo asks.

I sift through the last box that I am unpacking. "No, it's not."

Hands on hips, Rodrigo taps his foot impatiently. "Shit. I'm going to have to run out and buy more."

"Maybe I have what you're looking for?"

Rodrigo arches an eyebrow at me. "Oh no, sweetie. I highly doubt you would have a stash of condoms."

I blush, and shake my head. Condoms are definitely not something I have. He grabs his wallet off the kitchen counter and tells me he is running out to the nearest pharmacy to pick up a couple of boxes.

It's been a week since Rodrigo and I graduated from Boston University, and moved to New York City. We spent the past week unpacking and setting up our new home. We live in a charming two bedroom apartment in Chelsea that Rodrigo's parents had purchased. The apartment has high ceilings, and large windows. There are two bedrooms. Rodrigo offered the master bedroom to me, but since his parents are the owners I let him take it instead. The kitchen is not large, but it's enough room for both us to be in there at the same time. European cabinetry and stainless steel appliances dress it up. I wanted to contribute by giving Rodrigo's father some rent money each month; however, he refused. He thinks of me as his other daughter and will not take any money from me. I am truly blessed to have such wonderful people in my life.

On Monday, Rodrigo and I start our new jobs. I will be working for one of the most prominent real estate development companies in the nation, and Rodrigo will be working for a young clothing line that designs men's underwear, and sleepwear.

Luck was definitely on my side when I landed the job. The Blake Group was at the college career fair and I gave them my resume. The recruiter, who happened to be quite pretty and couldn't have been that much older than me, glanced at my resume. She asked a plethora of questions, and I answered as best as I could during the informal interview. She had been impressed with me, and a few days later I received a call to set up an online interview. The interview went successfully well, and earned me an entry position with the company. It wasn't the position I had hoped for, but it's a start.

~ * ~

The sound of my alarm clock goes off at seven. *Five more minutes.* I hit the snooze button. When the alarm goes off again, I stretch and slowly rise out of bed to shower. The steamy hot shower feels good and wakes me up. Once I finish showering, I brush my teeth, pull my hair into a neat chignon bun, apply my make-up, and head back to my room to dress.

I pick out a brand new beige skirt suit and a sleeveless draped silk black top pairing it with my favorite nude pumps. I check myself in the mirror one last time to make sure I look presentable on my first day. I grab my zippered leather portfolio and purse, and get ready to leave. A note is taped to the back of the door.

Cari,
Have a fantastic first day.
Love you,
R

I send him a quick text thanking him, and wish him a good first day as well. The subway ride to work is about half an hour, and then it's a short walk from the subway station to the soaring glass building where the Blake Group offices are. Sunlight streams through the glass panes and onto the gleaming marble floors in the enormous lobby. Past the reception desk there is a large sitting area where benches and chairs are surrounded by lush tropical plants, and a large water wall. I make my way to the reception desk.

"Good morning miss. How may I help you?" I look at her name tag.

"Good morning, Letisha. I'm Cari Snow. It's my first day here."

She smiles warmly at me. "Welcome to BG, Ms. Snow. You're going to love it here."

"Thank you. I was told I have to see Myra Dominguez."

"Sure. Let me announce your arrival." She picks up the phone and informs the person on the other end of my arrival. I observe how busy the lobby is as people head in to start their day.

"Ms. Snow?"

I turn back around. "Yes?"

"Here is your pass to get up to the offices. HR will have your employee badge ready for you by the end of today. You may proceed through the security gate after you have shown them your pass." She points to the gated off section where there is someone assigned to check everyone's badge. "Take the elevator to the thirty-fifth floor. Alana will be there to meet you."

"Thank you."

"You're welcome. Have a nice day."

"Thanks."

I hold up my pass up as I approach the security guard. He glances at me, and then my badge before letting me through. I walk to the elevator bank. There are six elevators, three on each side. One side stops at floors two through twenty only. The other side stops at floors twenty-one through thirty-five. When elevator number five arrives, I cram into the elevator. People are shouting out which floor they need to get off on and the button is pressed. There is complete silence on the ride up, and the smell of coffee makes my mouth water. Most of the passengers exit on the thirty-first floor, and I press the button for my trip to the thirty-fifth floor. It is a quick ride up and as soon as I step off a young pretty blonde lady greets me.

"Hi. Are you Carilyn Snow?"

"Yes. Please call me Cari."

"Welcome Cari. I'm Alana, the office manager." She offers me a handshake.

"It's very nice to meet you," I say shaking her hand.

"Likewise," she reciprocates.

"I have the pleasure of giving you the grand tour of our offices today, and getting you settled in."

"Great. Thank you."

Alana leads me through the automatic sliding glass doors. I look at both the right and left sides of the floor. The entire floor is mainly comprised of cubicles. Behind a row of cubicles are offices. Each office has glass walls and doors with name plates on the outside. Alana takes a right turn and points to each department introducing me to some of my new co-workers along the way.

She explains the floor is divided into the north wing and the south wing. The north wing only houses the offices of the executive board, and everyone else is in the south wing. "I sit here." Alana points to her cluttered desk, and then walks over to the next cubicle. "And your desk is right behind mine."

I notice each desk had an iMac and an iPad. Wow.

"Myra's office is behind you." She points to the office behind the glass wall where my boss sits. The office has a desk and a chair in it with plenty of natural lighting flowing in through the window. "She's in a meeting right now. You'll meet her later."

Alana suggests I put my bag away before we continue with the tour, and I do so. The floor is like an intricate maze. I will need a navigation system to find my way around. When I return to my desk, my boss is back in her office, and I finally get to meet Myra. She's very polished and well-spoken, but not too friendly. Alana had forewarned me that Myra is not pleasant, and can be intimidating. She's also gone through many assistants over the past year. I silently pray Myra will have some mercy on me. I don't want to lose this job.

~ * ~

DEVEN

Ten months ago, Dad was diagnosed with Alzheimer's disease. My father has always been my rock, and the man who I admire the most. He was the man who made sure I had the love of two parents after my biological mother left. The man who always made the time to support me at school and sport events. And now this incredible man is fighting a horrible memory robbing disease. Life can be so fucking unfair.

There had been early signs he had the disease, but none of us had known. My stepmother, sister, and I shrugged it off thinking he was just stressed, and needed a long overdue vacation. But then he began to make some poor business decisions, and became increasingly disoriented. He had occasional foul moods, and sometimes did not know who he was. It was then Mom and I suspected something was seriously wrong.

Together we brought him to his doctor who confirmed he was in the very early stages of Alzheimer's. The doctor cautioned us it would gradually get worse. It was devastating to hear this news. For weeks I dedicated a lot of my time to research the disease. I didn't know enough about Alzheimer's, and was desperate to find a way to try to help my father fight the disease, but my research proved futile. There was and is no cure for Alzheimer's.

In due course, Mom and I reluctantly admitted Dad to a care facility devoted to those with Alzheimer's. It was a difficult decision to make, but one that was necessary. We visit him as often as we can even though at times he has no inkling as to who we are.

A few months ago, the unthinkable happened. Dad suffered a stroke. It left him weak and his legs could no longer support him so he had to use a wheelchair in order to get around, but that was not the worst of it. The left side of his face was paralyzed and it made it impossible for him to eat and speak. Fortunately, the facility has a rehabilitation center making therapy accessible to him five days a week. His progress had been very slow and the doctors and therapists were no longer optimistic that the therapy would help him.

Fast forward to today and here I am preparing to officially take over my father's role as Chief Executive Officer. It is now my job to continue to maintain the company's success, and carry on Dalton Blake's legacy.

I am due at the lawyer's office at nine o'clock, and it has been a morning from hell with the street traffic. It's bumper to bumper leaving me no choice except to hop out of the cab and catch the subway which I very much despise. I arrive a few minutes late to the lawyer's office. He goes through everything and explains the process of what needs to be done. After signing all the necessary paperwork, I look down at my watch and see the time. I thank the lawyer, and rush out to hail a cab to John F. Kennedy airport so I can make my flight to California.

CHAPTER FOUR

June

DEVEN

It's good to be back in New York after spending the past few weeks in Los Angeles with Brad as we monitored the progress of our new offices, and moved forward with the next development project out there. I came into the office very early this morning so I can get a jump start on my work. My assistant, Catrina, left a stack of sorted files, and mail on my desk for me to go through. After spending a few hours clearing half of the files, I remove my glasses, and pinch the bridge of my nose. I have to meet with Jenna, the Director of Human Resources, to discuss changes I want made. On my way out of the office, I grab the file of signed documents for Catrina to process, but she's away from her desk. I drop the file on her desk and head towards the south side of the office. As I make my way to Jenna's office, I hear some gossiping coming from the break room.

"I think I'm going to ask that new chic out."

"Myra's new assistant?"

"Yeah. She's smoking hot."

"For sure. What I wouldn't do just to cop a feel of her."

"I know, right?"

They both laugh. I heard enough. It's time to make my appearance. I enter the room and see Jeremy and Oliver, financial analysts who report to Brad.

"Good morning gentlemen."

"Hello, sir. How are you today?" Jeremy asks sitting tall in his chair.

Yeah, yeah, kiss my ass. He's a fucking brown noser, and I loathe brown nosers. I cross my arms and scowl at the both of them. "Don't you two have work to do?"

"Uh, yes sir we do. As a matter of fact, we were just heading back," Jeremy says nervously.

"Good."

I watch the two of them scurry out. So Myra has another new assistant. She must have started while I was in Los Angeles. Dad had always made it a point to personally meet and greet each employee in his company, and I intend to continue this tradition. Think I'll take a detour past Myra's department first. Myra is great at her job as Director of Real Estate Development, but has a hard time keeping her assistants around. Since Myra joined the BG team five years ago, she has gone through ten assistants. The previous assistant lasted all of one week. It will be interesting to see how long this assistant will last.

~ * ~

CARI

My on-time performance to work ended this morning thanks to a sick passenger on the subway. I showed up an hour late to the departmental meeting. Myra did not look pleased when I entered the boardroom. If looks could kill, I'd be dead already.

After the meeting, I stop by the break room to get a cup of coffee. While I'm stirring the sugar in my coffee, I listen in on the conversation some of the office girls are having. Deven Blake is back. Alana had made me aware that Deven has recently taken over his father's position as CEO. I have yet to meet him. The girls talk about how good he looks, and gossip about his dating life. I throw away the stirrer, grab my coffee, and walk out. I am about three feet away from my desk when someone bumps into the back of me making my coffee splash onto my dress.

"Oh, no," I say to myself. This really has not been a good morning. I hurry to my desk to put the cup down, and grab some tissues to wipe off the stain.

"I beg your pardon."

I turn around and lift my head to see a pair of striking blue eyes gaze intensely at me. There's only been one time in my life when someone has looked at me with such intensity. As I'm finally able to focus on his face my chest tightens. *It can't be.*

"Cari?"

It is him. Holy crap! It's the hot guy from Club XTC. *And he remembers me.* My stomach is in knots, and my knees feel as if they're about to buckle. I take in the sight of the magnificent man in front of me from head to toe. He's still gorgeous, but he looks slightly different. His hair is not tied up like it was when I last saw him. He's wearing his brown chin-length hair down, and resembles a runway model for men's European designer suits. He's dressed in a crisp white French-cuffed shirt with a navy pin dot tie, and dark blue pinstriped pants all tailored perfectly to him.

He notices the stain on my dress. "Did I do that to your dress when I bumped into you?"

"It's fine. I'll send it to the cleaners."

"I'm so sorry. Please allow me pay to have your dress cleaned."

"I see you two have met," Alana says as she comes towards us.

"Actually –" He's cut off by Alana when she sees the stain.

"What happened to your dress?"

"It's my fault. I accidentally bumped into her while she had a cup of coffee in her hand."

"You're going to have to pay to have her dress dry cleaned Deven."

My eyes enlarge. Did she just call him Deven?

"I have already offered." He looks back at me. "Whatever the cost is I will take care of it. If the stain cannot be removed I promise to reimburse you for the dress. Are you Myra's new assistant?"

"Yes."

"We haven't been properly introduced. I'm Deven Blake." He extends his hand to me for a handshake.

Oh. My. God. *He* is Deven Blake. *He's the CEO. And I'm his employee.* Can this be any more awkward? I place my hand in his and shake it. Touching him again sends shivers through my body.

"Cari Snow," I say.

His eyes twinkle, and then the sexiest dimpled smile I have ever seen appears on his face leaving me breathless.

"It's a pleasure to finally meet you," he says as his hand is still clasped to mine.

"Did you two already know each other?" Alana asks looking back and forth between us.

"Not really," Deven replies as he releases my hand.

Alana seems befuddled, but neither of us offers an explanation.

"Welcome to BG, Cari. I am elated to have you here, and I'm sure you will be an asset to the company."

Oh for goodness sake, why do I have to blush in front of him?

"I've got to get to a meeting, but I'll see you around. Make sure I get the bill for the dress."

He winks at me and shows off that sexy dimpled smile again before turning to Alana. "See you later Alana." She waves to him, and he goes on his way.

"All the office girls are crazy about him. Even some of the guys."

"He's very nice to look at."

"Yes, he is. Great. Here comes the wicked witch of the south." She's referring to Myra. "You better get to work before she says anything."

"Chat at lunch?"

"You got it." Alana goes back to her desk.

I slide my chair in and get back to work.

CHAPTER FIVE

DEVEN

Meetings and video conference calls have forced me to keep my distance from Cari the entire week, but my thoughts have been constantly consumed by her. In fact, I've never been able to forget her since that night. She is the only girl I've ever been hung up on. She's even more beautiful than I remember her to be, and those almond-shaped jade green eyes of hers are fucking amazing. I can get lost in her eyes.

I looked over the file that I snatched from Human Resources. *Carilyn Jade Snow*. There is not much in her file besides her application, resume, credit report, and the results of her drug test. The one thing that stood out was that she graduated summa cum laude from Boston University. A beauty with brains. The kind of girl I want to get to know if it wasn't for the rule.

I glance down at the time on my Rolex. Time to go. I have to stop at Tiffany's to pick out a gift for my baby sister. I call Mauricio to have him meet me in front of the building. Clearing off my desk I take a couple of files with me to work on over the weekend. I stroll to the elevator and am surprised to see Cari. Why is she first leaving now? The office closes at noon every Friday during the summer. It's a policy my father implemented years ago as an incentive to all the employees for the hours they put in during the rest of the year.

"Why hello, Cari." God damn, she is sexy. I admire the way her jeans hugs her fine ass.

She peers up at me. "Oh, hi, um, Mr. Blake. I didn't know you were still here." She sounds nervous. Do I make her nervous?

"First of all, let's lose the Mr. Blake. Just call me Deven. And second of all, why are you still here?"

There's fear in her eyes like she is afraid of getting in trouble if she tells me. It must have something to do with Myra.

"You can tell me. You don't have to worry about ratting on someone. It will be between us."

She chews on her bottom lip debating whether or not to tell me.

"You'll keep it confidential?"

"You have my word."

She bows her head. "Myra needed me to finish a time sensitive assignment."

Just as I thought. "And what exactly was this time sensitive assignment?"

"She wanted all the meeting minutes from the beginning of the year to be typed up."

Myra had ample time to have those minutes typed, submitted to HR, and e-filed. *I'm onto you Myra.*

"So the minutes are all typed then?"

"Yes. It's done, and sent to her for review as she requested."

"I see. Well, thank you for staying behind to complete it."

"No problem."

The elevator beeps signaling its arrival. I let her enter first. The elevator stops on a couple of more floors, and we speak briefly about our week until we arrive on the main floor. I step aside to let Cari off. She wishes me a nice weekend right before we exit the building. I watch as she starts to walk away. What the fuck am I doing? Am I just going to let her walk away again? Fuck it. *To hell with my rule.*

"Cari, wait."

She comes to a halt and turns around. I catch up to her, and nervously rub the back of my neck. Why the hell am I feeling nervous all of a sudden? "Do you have plans for the remainder of the afternoon?" *Please say no.*

She tilts her pretty head to the side and hesitates. Shit, she has plans. Of course she does. It's Friday after all. She might even have a boyfriend and a date to get ready for.

"Not really."

I can barely conceal my surprise at her response. I clear my throat. "I have to go shopping at Tiffany's for my sister's birthday present, and could use some help. I'd like for you to come and help me pick something out for her."

"Oh, um…I'm not an expert in choosing birthday presents, but I'll be happy to try to help you." And the prettiest smile I have ever seen lights up that angelic face of hers. My afternoon just got so much better.

"Great. Come on."

~ * ~

CARI

Deven leads the way to the shiny black Mercedes parked in front of the building. We are going to be driven to Tiffany's? Seriously? The store is only a few blocks away. Surely we can walk.

"Good afternoon Deven." A middle-aged gentleman dressed in a suit opens the door for Deven, but Deven steps to the side allowing me to get in first.

"Good afternoon ma'am." The chauffeur gives me a nod.

I smile at him and get into the car sinking into the luxurious leather seats. Deven gets into the car from the other side, and instructs his chauffeur to take off.

My plan was to go home and relax after work. Maybe read a book. Instead, I am sitting in a fancy car with the CEO being driven to Tiffany's. I can't help myself from stealing a glance at him while his attention is on his phone. He can grace the cover of *GQ* with his well-defined chin, his perfectly straight nose, and his hypnotizing crystal blue eyes. And his hair. Oh my. He has gorgeous hair. How I would love to run my fingers through those strands of his.

Deven suddenly turns to face me and catches me gawking at him. My cheeks rapidly flame red, and I avert my gaze to my folded hands resting on my lap.

"We sort of got off to a strange start. I know it's too late, but I would still like to apologize for coming on to you so strongly at the club. I can't explain it, but the second I saw you I felt a very strong attraction to you. And I got caught up in the moment and lost all etiquette when I kissed you without even knowing anything about you other than your name." He runs a hand through his hair. "That's never happened before."

I wanted him to kiss me, and I clearly made no attempt to stop him. He wasn't the only one who got caught up in that moment.

"You have nothing to apologize for. I could have pushed you away, but I didn't. I felt a strong attraction to you too."

"The guy you were dancing with that night. Was he your boyfriend?"

I danced with only one other guy that night. I shake my head. "No. He's my best friend."

His mouth curves into a smile. Should I ask if he is still seeing that girl from the club? I gather my nerves and go for it. "Um, how is your girlfriend?"

His brows furrow. "Girlfriend?" He angles his head back and laughs. "Oh, she was definitely not my girlfriend. She was just someone that wouldn't leave me alone."

"So, no girlfriend?"

He shakes his head. "No girlfriend then, and no girlfriend now. Are you currently in a relationship?"

"No." If only he knew how long it's been since I last had a relationship.

"We don't really know a thing about each other yet there's this strong attraction between us. Do you think it's insane to feel this way?"

I shrug. "I don't know. It's never been like this for me."

"Me neither." He places his hand over my folded hands and my entire body tingles from his touch. "But I would like to get to know you."

I'm dumbfounded. "You want to get to know me?"

He smiles his perfect dimpled smile. "Yes, I believe that's what I said."

Staring down at our hands, German's words come back to me. *You deserve to be happy.*

"What do you say Cari?"

"I'd like that." I want to get to know him too.

He lifts my hand to his lips and presses a tender kiss to it. "And I want you to get to know me." How did he know what I was thinking? "I promise we'll start over and take it slow this time."

I nod and glance out the window. If this is a dream I never want to wake up. His fingers caress my cheek.

"You okay?"

I turn back to him, and smile reassuringly. "Yes. What do you plan on getting your sister for her birthday?"

"I'm not sure. What would you suggest?"

"How old will she be?"

"She'll be eighteen in a few short weeks."

I have no clue what his sister is like or what kind of taste she has. What piece of jewelry would be suitable for an eighteen year old girl? It should be something she can show off. "What about a bracelet?"

He's mulling over my suggestion. "A bracelet...yes, I think she would love a bracelet."

The ride to Tiffany's took longer than it would have had we walked. The car pulls up to the front of the store and Deven hops out of the car while his chauffeur comes around to open my door. Deven offers his hand to help me out of the car. He's such a gentleman, and I can really get used to having my hand in his. Not letting go of my hand we walk into the store, and I notice a few women stealing glances at him.

Deven brings me to the sterling silver jewelry. One of the associates shows us a selection of bracelets. He asks me for my opinion on each one before he finally settles on the signature bracelet with a heart shaped "Return to Tiffany" pendant.

"Thank you for coming with me to help choose her present," he says as we leave Tiffany's.

"No problem."

"Since we both haven't had lunch, would you like to get something to eat?"

I don't' realize how hungry I am until my stomach starts to rumble at the mention of lunch. "Lunch sounds real good right now."

"There's a burger joint I like down the street. Are you up for that?"

"That sounds good."

"Let me tell Mauricio we'll be walking there." I wait while he makes the call.

"Shall we?" he asks as he puts his phone away and holds out his hand. I slide my hand into his and he pulls me closer to him as we walk down the street.

"I hope your sister likes her gift."

"I'm sure she will. Do you have any siblings?"

"No. I'm an only child."

"Must have been nice to have all the attention to yourself."

I shake my head. "It was different for me. I lived with my grandparents. They raised me."

He comes to a stop and I almost stumble over my own feet.

"If you don't mind my asking, why did your grandparents raise you instead of your parents?"

"My mother died when I was an infant, and I don't know who my father is."

His free hand comes in contact with my face. My eyelids flutter as his thumb gently strokes my cheek. "I'm real sorry to hear that. It must have been hard growing up not knowing them."

"When I was younger it was hard. None of the kids understood why I did not have a mommy and daddy. They thought my parents didn't want me, but the older I got the more I realized how lucky I was that I had my doting grandparents bring me up. I could have ended up in an orphanage or in foster homes."

"You were fortunate." He tugs on my hand gently and we cross the street to The Burger Stand. The restaurant is known for their variety of gourmet organic burgers. This is my first visit here, but I've heard people in the office rave about it.

"Good afternoon, Mr. Blake," the hostess says flashing her pearly whites.

"Good afternoon, Monica. Two please. Preferably something in the back corner."

Her pearly white smile fades when she notices me. She seats us at a table in the back of the restaurant. Deven pulls out the chair for me. I thank him and he goes around to his chair.

"Enjoy," she says gazing at Deven.

Our waiter comes over to hand us menus and informs us of today's specials. We order our beverages first. I look over the menu, and my eyes double in size at the sight of the prices. The least expensive burger on the menu is twenty dollars. This is the most expensive hamburger I will ever eat. When our waiter returns to our table with our drinks he asks if we are ready to place our orders. I order the least expensive burger while Deven orders some fancy name burger.

"I tried going after you the night you left the club in a hurry." He frowns. "I had all the security cameras checked, but no one knew who you were."

I lower my head and play with the fold on my napkin. "That's because it was my first time there. And I only ran out because your girlfriend showed up."

He lifts my chin up. "I told you earlier, she was not my girlfriend. Have you been back to the club since?"

I shake my head. "No. We were only there that one night to celebrate my birthday."

"Your birthday?"

"Yes."

He takes out his phone. "So your birthday is…" He's tapping his chin trying to guess the date.

I help him out. "It's May twenty-second."

"And you turned…"

"I turned twenty-three last month."

"Well, happy belated birthday."

"Thank you." I lean back in my chair. "Now that I've told you when my birthday is I think it's only fair you tell me when yours is."

"Quite fair." His brilliant blue eyes search mine. "And feel free to ask anything of me Carilyn."

I look at him in shock. "How did you know my full name is Carilyn?"

"It's my business to know everything about my employees. And the answer to your question is June eleventh."

"So you're now twenty-six." His eyebrows arch. Uh-oh. I had not meant for that to slip. I only discovered his age when I had gone on Google to search for information on him.

"I see you know my age."

I cover my face in embarrassment. I am so stupid for blurting that out. His warm hands pry mine off my face.

"I don't want you to cover that beautiful face of yours."

"I'm so embarrassed. I didn't mean – "

"Embarrassed about what? It's not a crime to know my age unless you think I'm too old for you."

"No! Not at all." I feel the heat rush to my cheeks.

"Good." He reaches for his glass. "Happy belated birthday Cari. I wish I could have celebrated with you last year and last month, but I am happy that we have been brought together again so we can celebrate it now. And I look forward to celebrating many more birthdays with you."

So do I.

CHAPTER SIX

DEVEN

I bite into my burger and glance at the angel in front of me as she takes a bite of her burger. She closes her eyes for a few seconds as she chews, and it makes my dick wake up. Shit. She opens her eyes and catches me staring at her. I clear my throat.

"How is your burger?"

"It's very good."

I like that she is having a burger and fries and not a salad. Salads are not meals.

"That color looks really pretty on you. What color is it? Natural?" I take a sip of my drink.

"It's nude."

I choke on my drink.

"Oh my God! Are you alright?" Her voice is full of concern. I hold my hand up and nod. I point to my throat, drink some water, and clear my throat.

"Swallowed too fast." I continue to clear my throat again a few more times until I am able to speak again. "I'm sorry about that. Is that really a color?"

"Yes. It's a neutral color and goes well with just about any other color. It so happens to be my favorite color. What about you? Do you have a particular color you like?"

I lean back and cross my arms. I never really had a favorite color per se, but I do favor gray a lot. "I would say it's gray."

"Gray is a very complementing color."

I know nothing of complementing colors, and move onto the next question I have on my mind.

"Tell me what your favorite cuisine is."

"I love Thai food."

"Me too." It really is my favorite. And I have the perfect Thai restaurant I would like to take her to next time.

"Favorite movie?"

"*Twilight*."

Ugh! What is it with girls and that stupid vampire movie? Who could have guessed a story about a fucking immortal and a human could be so popular?

She tilts her head. "Now it's your turn to tell me what your favorite movie is."

"Don't have a favorite." It's the truth. My turn again. "Favorite book?"

"*Twilight*."

How did I not see that one coming?

"Is your sister your only sibling?"

"No. I have a half-brother, and half-sister that live in California."

"I always wondered what it would have been like to have a sibling, but having my best friend around is like having a sibling."

"I know what you mean."

"You must have a best friend then."

"I do. He's like a brother to me. In fact, you may have met him…Brad Wong. He's the CFO of the company."

"I heard his name before, but I don't think I have met him yet."

"If you met him, you wouldn't forget him. He hits on beautiful women all the time. You'll see when you meet him." Her cheeks are tainted pink. Is she not accustomed to hearing such compliments?

We exchange stories on how we met our best friends, and then talk about our time in college. She tells me how she lost her grandmother right before Christmas during her second year in college. How awful it must be to lose someone you love right before the holiday. I truly admire her for despite her loss she finished college.

I ask her about her career aspiration and learn that she wants to work in the social media industry. She would like to someday have her own web design business. If only I had need for another person in my social media department it would give her a start, and I would not hesitate to transfer her in a blink of an eye.

This has been by far the most enjoyable lunch I have had in a very long time. I look down at my watch. The afternoon has slipped by so quickly. I'm not ready to let her go yet, and need to quickly come up with a plan to keep her out a little longer.

"It's a bit early, but would you like to go for a cappuccino? I know a great coffee shop in SoHo that makes the best cappuccino."

"Cappuccino sounds great."

Yes! "Good. By the way, I never received the dry cleaning bill for your dress."

"Um, I took care of it."

"Cari, it's the least I could do for ruining such a pretty dress."

"It's fine. It was not that expensive to have it cleaned."

I want to make it up to her for ruining her dress and make a mental note to myself to buy her a new dress. I motion to the server for our bill. He immediately comes over and hands the bill to me.

"Please let me know how much my share is." She pulls out her wallet and opens it.

What? I've never had a girl offer to pay even if it was just for her share. No frigging way am I letting her pay. "I appreciate your offering, but this is on me."

"That's generous of you, but I can't let you pay for me."

I held up one hand. "Yes, you can. It was I who invited you to lunch. Please allow me."

"That's very kind of you. Thank you."

"It's my pleasure Cari." I take out my wallet and leave the money for the server. "Shall we go and have our cappuccinos?"

"Yes."

I call Mauricio to come pick us up. By the time we leave the restaurant,

Mauricio is in the car waiting for us. I open the door for Cari, and then I slide in beside her. I reach for her hand holding it in mine until we arrive at the coffee shop.

The coffee shop is crowded, but I know the manager and after exchanging a few pleasantries he seats us at a table in the back. I don't need to look at the menu, and watch Cari as she peruses the menu. Before I could ask what she is planning on getting our waitress comes over.

"Hello, my name is Darlene. What can I get you two?" Darlene asks me first.

I look at Cari. "Ladies first."

"I'd like the house mocha cappuccino please."

"Sure, and what can I get for you sir?" Darlene asks not once turning around to look at Cari when she gave her order. I will speak to the manager about her later.

"I'll have the house mocha cappuccino as well."

"Absolutely. Be back shortly with your cappuccinos." She winks at me, and goes to put in our order.

~ * ~

CARI

I don't believe the waitress was just staring at him like he's a piece of juicy steak. He is juicy, but he already has company – me. Why am I bothered by her reaction to him?

"Are you okay?"

We're just two people getting to know each other, but the words come out of my mouth before I can stop them. "Wow. She couldn't take her eyes off of you."

He shrugs. "Can't help it. I'm not interested in her," he says matter-of-factly as our eyes lock.

I should not have said that, and change the subject.

"Did you see yourself becoming a CEO so soon?"

"No, I did not. It wasn't supposed to happen so soon."

There seems to be more to his response. "What do you mean?"

He doesn't answer right away. "My father has Alzheimer's."

The news takes me by surprise. "I'm sorry Deven. When was he diagnosed with Alzheimer's?"

"We found out about ten months ago, but unfortunately the disease had unexpectedly progressed rather rapidly. It got harder for Mom to take care of him at home, and we had to admit him into a care facility for Alzheimer's patients. It wasn't an easy decision to make."

"I can't imagine it was."

"No, you can't. We didn't have a choice. Then he suffered a stroke not too long after, and he's never been the same." His blue eyes cloud with sadness.

I know first-hand how difficult it is to watch someone you love slowly wither away. "This must be difficult for you and your family."

"It is. No one in the company knows about my father. They are all under the impression he wanted to retire early. This is a very personal matter to me, and the only other person outside family that knows is Brad, and now you."

I want him to know he can trust me. "I would never tell anyone." I lay my hand over his to reassure him. He places his other hand on top of mine and gives it a squeeze.

The waitress comes back with our cappuccinos. After placing our cups down in front of us, she leans forward to Deven practically shoving her cleavage in his face. How brazen!

"Is there anything else I can get for you?" Darlene asks batting her eyelashes at him.

"No, thank you," he says not even giving her a second glance. She smiles at him, hands him the check, and winks at him before walking away. I have to fight the temptation to roll my eyes.

Moving the conversation away from his father, we talk about where we grew up and our childhood. Deven grew up in Greenwich, Connecticut. His father raised him alone when his biological mother left them. He does not mention why his mother left and it's too early in this stage to ask.

"It's almost eight. I hate for this night to end, but I do have to head home and finish up some work."

We've been talking like we've known each other for years and I wished we had more time. "I understand. Thank you Deven for everything today."

"No, thank you. I appreciate your help with the gift, and you certainly made the rest of my day so much more pleasurable. I'll have Mauricio drive you home."

"There's no need to. I can take the train back."

"No. I'd feel better if he drives you home."

"Alright then."

He calls Mauricio and as expected his car is outside waiting for us when we exit the coffee shop. Mauricio asks me for my address and I give it to him. The drive to my apartment is quick, and Deven escorts me to the lobby door.

"Thanks again for dinner, and for the cappuccino."

"My pleasure. I'd like to do this again soon."

"I'd like that too."

"Great. I guess I'll see you on Monday then."

"Yeah. See you Monday."

"Enjoy your weekend."

"You too."

Neither of us move, and we both laugh.

"Why don't you go in first? I want to know you're safely inside before I leave."

"Okay." I unlock the door.

"Wait."

I spin back around and he's standing inches from me. I inhale the delicious scent of him. He leans in and gives me a kiss on the cheek.

"Good night Cari," he whispers.

"Good night Deven."

I walk into the lobby and look back to see him wave to me before getting into his car.

CHAPTER SEVEN

CARI

"Wake up sunshine!"

My mattress dips forcing me to roll over to the other side of my bed.

"Sweetie, it's time to rise and tell."

I groan. "What is there to tell?"

"I want you to tell me who you were with last night."

I open my eyes immediately. "How did you know?"

"Hunter and I saw you with some hot guy last night when we turned the corner to come back here." Hunter is Rodrigo's boyfriend who made the transition to New York City with us.

I roll back over. "You were spying on me?"

"Not really. So are you going to tell me or do I have to drag it out of you?"

Patience is not one of Rodrigo's virtues. I tell him about my afternoon with Deven making sure I leave out the part about his father having Alzheimer's. Rodrigo knew Deven and I had bumped into each other earlier in the week, but he thought it was a dead issue when Deven did not make an effort to talk to me the rest of the week.

"This is so exciting! It's like Prince Charming finally finding Cinderella!"

"This is not a fairy tale."

"I know sweetie, but it's almost like one. What is he like?"

"He's caring, smart, generous, and gorgeous."

"See? He is Prince Charming."

I push my hair away from my forehead. "And how was your date with

Hunter?"

"Nice. We had dinner, and caught a movie."

"No clubbing?"

"No. We came to a decision to frequent the clubs less now."

"Oh?"

"Hunter and I want to travel instead. Maybe go on some weekend trips, and save for an exotic vacation."

"Did someone call for me?"

"Hi Hunter."

"Good morning sunshine," Hunter says bending down to give me a cheek to cheek kiss.

Hunter is a great looking guy, and also my other BFF. This former Cali native has long blonde hair that grazes his shoulders, slate-colored eyes that hook you in, and a great muscular tan body. Paired with my dark haired, hazel-eyed, muscular best friend they are a perfect match not only physically, but also emotionally. They balance each other so well. Rodrigo has never lasted more than two weeks with any of his former partners. Hunter is the exception. Four months together and they are still going strong.

"What were you two saying about me?"

"I was just telling her about our decision to go away on weekends."

"You should come with us Cari."

"She may not be able to."

"Why not?"

"She has a boyfriend."

"Rodrigo is stretching the truth. I do not have a boyfriend. We're just getting to know each other."

"Who is he?"

"He's the CEO of the company, but she met him briefly last year."

Hunter is baffled and I bring him up to speed on how Deven and I first met.

"I am so happy you are finally moving on," Rodrigo tells me.

"It's a good step forward Cari."

"I think he may want to see me again."

"He would be a fool if he didn't want to."

"He's right Cari. Any heterosexual man would be stupid to let a sexy and gorgeous lady like you get away from him, and twice at it."

My best friends have such a way of inflating my ego. I love having them in my life. Rodrigo wraps me in a tight hug. "Love you sweetie."

"Love you back."

"What do you say to going out for breakfast?" Hunter asks.

"Sounds good," I reply.

Rodrigo hops off my bed and leaves with Hunter to get ready. I reach for my phone on my nightstand and see I have a couple of text messages. I don't recognize the number, but open the messages anyway. The messages are from Deven. How did he get my cell phone number? He's the CEO. He can get anything he wants. I save his number to my phone, and read each message.

> D: Thank you for a most enjoyable afternoon
> and evening.

I read the next text.

> D: Do you have any plans next Saturday?

A smile erupts on my face, and my heart does a happy dance. He does want to see me again. I quickly type my response to him.

> Me: No plans for Saturday.

I put my phone down, and run a brush through my hair. I open up my drawers to look for a change of clothes, and pull out a pair of cut-off shorts and a baby tee. I change and go to the bathroom to brush my teeth.

Before we leave, I check my phone again and there is another text message from him.

> D: May I take you out on a date Saturday?

I can't believe it! Gorgeous and sexy Deven Blake wants to take me out on a date. I send my reply.

> Me: Yes.

"Wow. Look at that smile on your face. It must be from Deven," Rodrigo says.

"It is."

"I haven't seen you smile like that over a guy in like forever," Rodrigo adds. "What did he say?"

"He's taking me out next Saturday."

Rodrigo claps his hands. "Whoo-hoo! That's wonderful!"

"It is. Okay, I'm starving. Let's go and Cari can fill us in over breakfast," Hunter says rubbing his stomach.

The three of us walk down the corridor and pass by an apartment with its door open.

"Looks like we have a new neighbor," Rodrigo says stopping and peering into the new apartment. "We should say hello and introduce ourselves."

Hunter rolls his eyes and faces me. "I guess his parents never taught him not to talk to strangers."

His comment makes me giggle and Rodrigo scowls at the both of us. I purse my lips to stop me from giggling.

"Hello?" Rodrigo asks as he knocks on the door. There seems to be no one in the apartment so he takes a few steps in. "Hello?" Still no answer.

"Maybe your new neighbor stepped away."

"I guess so. Too bad. I wanted to meet our new neighbor, and extend a warm welcome to them."

"Plenty of time to do that," Hunter tells him as we continue our way to the elevator.

The elevator doors open, and a very nice looking guy steps off holding a box in his arms. He must be our new neighbor.

"Well, hello there," Rodrigo says making Hunter narrow his eyes at him. I suppress the urge to laugh.

"Oh, hello! I apologize for holding up the lift." Oh, he's British.

Rodrigo cocks his head to the side. "That's quite alright." He waves his hand. "We were not waiting that long. Is that your apartment with the door opened?"

"Yes, that's my flat."

"Welcome. It's very nice to meet you." Rodrigo offers a handshake. Our new neighbor puts down the box to shake his hand. "I'm Rodrigo. And this is Hunter, and Cari."

Nice looking guy shakes Hunter's hand first, and then mine. His hand seems to linger on mine. I gently pull my hand back.

"It's a pleasure to meet all of you. I'm Zach."

"Do you need help moving your boxes up?"

I peer up at Hunter and he's visibly annoyed. If Rodrigo does not stop talking soon, Hunter is going to drag him out of here by the collar.

"Thank you for the offer, but I have the last of the boxes here." He points down at the box. "I'd love to have you over and get to know all of you after I get settled."

"How kind of you! We'd love to come over. We live in apartment five twelve which is a little further down the hall."

Hunter's stomach growls.

"Oh, dear Lord. Control your hunger will you?"

"I can't. I'm starving."

"It was very nice meeting you. We'll see you around."

"Yeah. See you around."

I step into the elevator and turn around to find Zach's gaze on me. I swallow.

"I've seen him before," Rodrigo insists once the doors close.

"Oh really?" Hunter asks with a hint of sarcasm in his voice.

"I can't remember where though, but he looks awfully familiar. Anyway, I think you have an admirer Cari."

"Rodrigo, stop stirring the pot. She likes Deven."

"I'm not stirring any pot. She's not his girlfriend yet so she's free to look at the crop."

"You're making this more than what it is. He was staring at all of us. Maybe he's gay too."

Both of them shake their heads.

"Nah. He's definitely not gay."

"Gotta agree with your best friend on this."

"Let's just drop it, and go have a nice breakfast," I say.

"Very well then," Rodrigo says in a British accent.

Rolling my eyes I exit the elevator and lead the way to breakfast.

CHAPTER EIGHT

CARI

The start of the new week is a repeat of last week. Another sick passenger on the subway causes me to be late to work again. I quickly drop my purse off at my desk and run to the boardroom. Myra stops speaking when I walk into the room. All heads around the table turn to me.

"Ms. Snow, do you know what time it is?"

"Yes, ma'am. I'm sorry. There was a sick passenger on the tr-"

She crosses her arms. "I do not want to hear your excuse. My meetings begin on time. This is the second time you have shown up late to my meeting. I will not tolerate tardiness. If this happens one more time, I will write you up."

My face turns crimson. All I want to do is flee the room and stick my head in a hole. After the meeting I head into the stairwell and go down a couple of flights. I lean against the wall and release the tears I had been holding back after Myra humiliated me in front of my co-workers. I hear footsteps coming down the stairs, and quickly try to wipe away my tears.

"Cari?"

I freeze. Oh no. Is there no end to my humiliation today? I should have gone to the ladies restroom instead and lock myself in a stall.

Deven moves closer to me and cradles my face with his hands. "What's wrong?"

"It's nothing."

"I don't buy it Cari. Something has you upset. Tell me what it is."

I take in a deep breath and glance up the stairs fearing Myra will walk through the door any second and fire me for disappearing from my desk.

41

Deven follows my gaze and then returns his worried gaze to me.

He interlaces his fingers with mine. "Come with me."

"No. I can't leave. Myra will fire me."

He lets go of my hand and taps at the screen on his iPhone.

"Myra? Deven here. I'm pulling Cari away from you for a little bit. I need her assistance on a new project I have in mind." He pauses and I wonder what she's telling him. "Great. Thanks Myra." He taps at his screen and takes my hand once again.

We walk down to the next level and catch the elevator. He tugs on my hand as we stride out of the building and down a couple of blocks to Starbucks. He goes to order our coffee while I sit down at a table and wait.

"Your cinnamon dolce latte." He sets my drink down and sits in the chair across from me. "Now will you tell me what had you so upset?"

I swallow some of my coffee, and stare out the window. This is the second time I will be ratting on my boss. How can I avoid answering his question? He gingerly turns my face so I am looking at his gorgeous face.

"I would like to help you Cari if I can, but until you tell me what happened there's nothing I can do."

I bite my bottom lip and he tugs on it to free it.

"I walked into the meeting late again this morning, and in front of everyone she pointed out it was the second time I was late, and the next time will result in a write up."

His face remains impassive. "Why were you late?" He takes a sip of his latte.

"There was a sick passenger on the train and we had to wait until the paramedics came."

"Did Myra ask what happened?"

"No. She was quite condescending. It was humiliating."

The color of Deven's eyes changes to an icy blue. He pulls out his iPhone and makes a call.

"It's Deven." Pause. "I need for you to carve time on my calendar today. It is imperative I meet with Myra."

Oh my God!

"Good. Yes, it is compulsory. Thank you." He hangs up.

"You're going to talk to Myra about this?"

"That's right."

"You can't."

He regards me with a look that dares me to argue with him. "I can, and I will."

Seriously, can this day get any worse for me?

"She's going to fire me."

He leans forward and takes my hand in between his. "She will do no such thing. I'm a resourceful man Cari. The entire building is outfitted with cameras, and each boardroom has a camera in it. If I roll the video back, I will be able to see it for myself."

I am petrified. Crossing Myra is not a smart thing to do.

"You're trembling. Are you cold?" I shake my head. He traces circles on the top of my hand. "You're worried what she's going to do to you?"

"Yes," I whisper.

"You have nothing to worry about. Trust me, okay?"

I draw in a deep breath, and slowly give him a nod. I trust him. I have to.

~ * ~

DEVEN

I invite Cari back to my office after our morning coffee break.

"Please, have a seat." I push a button and the glass windows and door facing the corridor fog up obscuring the view into my office.

Cari sits down and crosses her lovely long legs. Hmm…I want those legs wrapped around me. *Concentrate Blake.*

"It's a very nice office you have here. Such a beautiful view of Central Park," she says as she takes in my enormous office.

She's mistaken. The beautiful view is sitting right in front of me. "Are you feeling a little better?"

"Yes, thank you." She flashes a radiant smile at me.

"Have dinner with me tonight?"

"Dinner sounds great."

"Perfect. I do have one request."

"And what's that?"

"Do not mention our dinner date to anyone in the office."

"I would not have said anything."

"Good. The office is full of gossipmongers, and I don't want you to be the subject of their petty gossip." The last thing Cari needs is for those jealous office girls to stir shit up.

I love talking to her and keep her in my office for nearly an hour before I let her get back to work.

"I'll call you later with a time for dinner."

"Okay."

I walk her to the door, but before she can open it I grab her hand. Bringing her hand to my lips I kiss the top of it. What I really want to do is kiss her, but I said I would take it slow. I open the door and walk with her down the hall. Bradley is speaking with Catrina when we reach the reception area. He does a double take at Cari, and then looks back at me with arched eyebrows.

"Cari?" She turns to me. "I'd like for you to meet Bradley Wu. He's our CFO. Brad, this is Cari Snow."

"Very nice to meet you Ms. Snow," Brad says shaking her hand.

"Nice to meet you as well Mr. Wu."

Brad is ogling her. Seriously? He's had enough time with her.

"Cari, you better go."

"Yes, I better." She offers me a smile and leaves.

I go back to my office and Brad follows me shutting the door behind him.

"Who was that beautiful lady? She looks so familiar."

I lean back in my chair. "That was Cari."

Brad scratches his head. "Cari?"

"The angel from Club XTC."

"The one you've been hung up on?"

"Yep." I grin.

"What was she doing here?"

I tell him she works for us now, and explain to him the events of last week.

"You've been holding out on me man."

"I was going to tell you eventually."

"So you're off the market?"

"I haven't been on the market in a while."

"She's very beautiful. She's got some nice titties too."

His comment makes me want to knock out his front teeth. "Keep your eyes off of her chest."

He puts his hands up. "I'm just sayin'."

"Well, she is very beautiful, but there's more to her. She's so different from the other shallow girls. She's well-educated, gracious, intelligent, and sweet." She exudes innocence and coyness that was absent from previous girls I'd been with.

"Intelligent? You don't do intelligent."

"I've always wanted to be with someone who has brains. I just never found someone until now. I think she's it for me."

Brad's eyes grow big. "You barely know her."

"On the contrary, I know more about her than the other girls I have gone out with combined. I'm telling you Brad, I have never met anyone like her. She's like a breath of fresh air. She's intriguing. And there's this indescribable connection between us. I've never felt it with anyone else."

Brad claps his hands and tosses his head back laughing. *Asshole.* "I don't fucking believe it. She's bewitched you."

He makes it sound like it's a bad thing. "So what if I am? Someday you'll know how it feels."

He shrugs. "Maybe in the far future."

I hold up Cari's file. "I pulled this from HR."

"What is it?" He takes the file and looks at the tab. "You have her personnel file?"

I give him a nod. Brad opens it, and looks at it.

"She graduated summa cum laude in her class? Beautiful, and smart. Perhaps you're right. Maybe she is the one for you."

"She is. I'm taking her to dinner tonight."

His eyebrows lift. "People around the office are going to stir up some shit if they see the two of you having dinner."

"I'm aware rumors may circulate so I asked her not to say anything. We'll have to be discreet about it."

Brad nods in agreement. "So did you see Ting's email? He has another building that might be of interest to us."

I want to put BG's global mark in Hong Kong, but the last deal I had fell through. It's one of my goals to have us there, and I am determined to keep at it until the company has set its footprints there.

"Yes, I saw it."

"What do you think?"

"I'm going to have to arrange to go there and see if for myself."

"What about L.A.?"

"You're going to have to go to L.A. instead."

"That's cool."

I'm glad I was able to convince Brad to move to New York and work at BG before we graduated college. I can always rely on him to represent the company and make good sound decisions in my absence. He has proven his worth time and again, and with his help, BG will become even more successful.

CHAPTER NINE

CARI

Myra gave me the silent treatment after her meeting with Deven. At five o'clock, she slammed her office door and left for the day. I'm looking forward to having dinner with Deven after the day I had. He suggested we leave the office separately and meet up at the restaurant.

The cab pulls up in front of Nobu. I reach into my purse to take out my wallet to pay, and am startled when the door opens.

"Hey," Deven says. "I'll take care of the fare."

"No, that's quite alright. I have my – "

"Cari, please." He holds out his hand and I take it. When I am out of the cab he gives me a tender kiss on the cheek.

"Come on. I don't have all day," the annoyed cab driver says.

"Right." Deven pulls a bill from his wallet and hands it to the cab driver. "Keep the change. Thank you for bringing her here safely."

"Thank you sir. You and your lovely lady enjoy your dinner." The cab driver smiles widely before pulling away.

"Thank you for paying my cab –"

He puts a finger over my lips sending delicious tingles up and down my body. "You have to stop thanking me. I would do anything for you." He kisses my forehead. Holy sweetness! Where has Deven been all my life? "Come. Our table is ready." He places his hand on the small of my back and holds open the door for me.

The hostess sees Deven and leads us to our table.

"How was the rest of your day?"

"It was somewhat bearable."

"Did Myra say anything to you?"

"No. She pretty much ignored me after she met with you."

"I'm sorry Cari, but I was not going to let her get away with what she did to you. Don't let her get under your skin."

Our server approaches our table and we order.

"I'm looking forward to spending Saturday with you." There goes that dimpled smile I love so much.

"So am I."

"I'd like to take you to Central Park."

"It's going to be a beautiful day to spend there."

"Yes, it will be. A beautiful day to spend with a beautiful girl."

I flush and look down at the linen napkin on my lap. I'm confounded by Deven's suggestion to go to Central Park. "How is this going to work?"

"What do you mean?"

"What if someone sees us together?"

"Are you worried?"

I nod and avert my gaze to my plate.

"Cari, look at me." I lift my head to find serious blue eyes regarding me. "Let me worry about it should that happen."

"Okay."

We speak about so many different things throughout dinner. It's so easy to talk to him. His chauffeur drives me back to my apartment and like last time, Deven walks me to the door.

"Dinner was delicious. Thank you." I cover my mouth realizing my slip.

He smiles and I know he caught my slip. "I enjoy taking you out to eat." He pushes back some of my loose hair, and his fingers linger on my face.

"It's been a while since I've been on a date."

He looks at me incredulously. "A while?"

My eyes peer up into his. "I haven't been on a date in a few years."

"I don't understand," he says shaking his head. "You're stunning."

And he will never need to understand. He cannot know about that part of my past. It was a terrible time in my life, and it's something that needs to remain buried. "It was my choice, and I rather not talk about it now."

"I understand, but I hope you will trust me enough soon to tell me." Sensing my discomfort, he changes the course of our conversation. "We should plan to secretly meet up for lunch at the park during the work week." He sounds like a little boy plotting to sneak out of the house, and it makes me giggle.

"I would love that, but I only have an hour for lunch. I'm sure my boss will be watching the clock."

He rubs his chin. "I'm sure I can convince your boss to let you have an extended lunch break."

"She's a tough one to convince."

"Remember who her boss is." He smirks. "I'm in and out of the office the rest of the week at meetings so I won't see you until Saturday. I'll come get you at eleven on Saturday?"

"Yeah. Eleven is perfect."

He's looking at me with those intense blue eyes of his. I want him to kiss me.

"See you then. Good night, Cari." He kisses me on the cheek again, and I hide my disappointment. I was hoping for a kiss on the lips.

"Good night, Deven."

"Go in so I know you're inside safely."

I go inside and head straight to the elevator. I walk into the apartment and lock the door. I throw my keys down on the kitchen counter, and go into the living room. Rodrigo is sitting on the couch with a pint of ice cream on his lap watching television.

"Hi."

"Hi sweetie! How was your day?"

I groan and plop myself down on the couch beside him.

"Oh, no. What happened?"

I recall today's events to him starting with my horrible commute. The only good thing that happened was having dinner with Deven.

"Your boss is such a bitch. She needs a good lay. Maybe then her attitude towards you will change." I let out a hearty laugh. "Now let's talk about that hot man of yours." He puts down his empty ice cream container on the coffee table and leans back.

"He's not my man."

"Sure, sure."

"We're not even dating yet. We're going out on our first date on Saturday."

"You've had dinner with him twice."

"I went for a late lunch with him on Friday, and tonight's dinner was a spur of the moment thing."

"Still a date."

"If he did not find me in the stairwell I would not have gone to dinner with him."

"Cari, you don't know if he would have asked you to have dinner with him."

"I don't think he would have. He's so busy. He already told me he won't be able to see me until Saturday." I look down at my fingernails.

"I think he's quite taken with you."

"You think so?"

"I know so."

"I'm nothing like the women he's been with."

"And what kind of women are those?"

"You know, the glamorous and gorgeous ones."

Rodrigo scrunches up his face. "Seriously Cari?"

"Have you seen them? There are a million pictures of him with beautiful women on the internet."

He waves his hands at me. "Hello? Stop doubting yourself. How many times do I need to remind you how gorgeous you are? You're one hundred percent genuine. Those other women he has been with all have had surgical enhancements, and they don't possess an ounce of brainpower." He puts an arm around me, and gives my shoulder a squeeze. "Let go of your insecurities, and be happy."

CHAPTER TEN

DEVEN

I feel like a teenager going on his first date. I hardly slept a wink last night excited to spend the day with her. I have never felt so giddy over a girl, but there's something about Cari. After my morning workout, I shower and dress which still left me with a lot of time. I catch up on some work until it's time I head into the City.

Mauricio gets me there fifteen minutes early and I wait patiently in the car. When it's one minute to eleven I jump out of the car and practically sprint to her building. I press the button located next to her apartment number and she buzzes me in. I ride the elevator to the fifth floor and walk down the corridor until I find her apartment. I can barely breathe when she opens the door. She is a vision of angelic beauty in her white sundress.

"Hi, beautiful," I say leaning in to kiss her cheek. She smells heavenly. Suddenly going to the park is the last thing I want to do.

"Hi. Come in." Cari steps back letting me inside her apartment.

I remember her telling me she lives here with her best friend, and wonder if he is around. "Is your best friend home?"

"No, he's not. He'll be back later. Can I get you something to eat or drink?"

"No, thank you. I had breakfast. Have you eaten this morning?"

Cari shakes her head. "I'm not really into breakfast. Coffee is usually my best friend in the morning."

I grimace. "Coffee is not food. You need to eat."

As quickly as one snaps their fingers, she changes the subject. "Can I give you a tour of the apartment?"

She is deliberately evading the subject of her eating breakfast. I'll drop it for now, but I will bring this up again later. Her health and well-being is important to me. "I'd love to see the apartment."

She starts off in the living room which is adequately furnished with a couch, an oversized chair, and a huge square coffee table. A large television sits on top of a cabinet. She moves on and shows me the kitchen. The apartment is much smaller than my place, but it is well-kept and cozy. We pass by a closed door and she takes me into the room next to it. It's her bedroom. Her room is simply furnished with a full size bed, a night table, and a dresser. There is a picture of an older couple on her night table.

"Is that a picture of your grandparents?"

"Yes. It's my favorite picture of them."

"You're lucky to have known your grandparents. I never knew mine."

"I'm sorry."

"Me too. It would have been nice to have known them. So, are you ready to go?"

She nods. "Let me grab my sweater, and bag."

I'm so fucking elated to be with her. I can't wait until she sees what I have planned for her later. She looks back at me and sees my gleaming smile.

"What are you smiling about?"

"I'm just very happy we are spending the day together."

"Me too."

She locks the door and I take her hand in mine as we walk towards the elevator.

"Mauricio will drive us to the park."

She lifts an eyebrow. "Are you opposed to mass transit?"

"I detest public transportation." Her eyes widen at my admission. What a stupid snobbish thing for me to say since she relies on public transportation to get around. "I don't like the subway nor the bus. I can tolerate cab rides, and commuter trains." There, much better.

The doors to the elevator open. I'm about to press the button for the first floor when I hear a male voice asking to hold the "lift." I hold out my arm to prevent the door from closing. I see him jogging towards the elevator. He gets in and thanks me. Then his eyes shift to Cari. I don't like the way he looks at her.

"Hello, Cari," he says in his British accent.

Apparently he already knows Cari.

"Hi, Zach."

I size the motherfucker up. He smiles at her and my free hand instantly curls into a fist.

"It's a lovely day. Are you spending it outdoors?"

"Yep. We're going to Central Park," Cari responds to him. "Oh gosh, where are my manners? Zach, this is Deven."

"It's nice to meet you Deven." He extends his hand and I reluctantly force myself to release my fist and shake his hand. "Cari, did you check with your roomie to see which day you would like to come over for lunch?"

What? She's going to his place? Before Cari can answer his question, the doors open. He steps off first. I walk behind Cari keeping our hands entwined.

"Rodrigo never got back to me. I will check with him again." Over my dead body.

"Sounds good. Have a lovely day at Central Park." He leaves the building first. Thank God.

"You're not really going to go over to his apartment are you?"

"Why not?"

Either he has already charmed her, or she is too innocent to know what he fucking has in mind.

"Because that guy wants nothing except to get you into his bed." Her eyes widen and her cheeks are red. "I don't trust him."

Her brows come together. "But you don't know him."

"Do you?"

"We're just doing the neighborly thing. I won't be going solo. Rodrigo will be there too." Am I supposed to be relieved that he will be there too? Absolutely not. I saw the way he looked at her. He's a shark circling his prey. He wants her.

"Cari, I don't think it's a good idea."

She looks at me with those incredible green eyes of hers. "Don't you trust me?"

"I trust you. I just don't trust him."

"Would you like me to ask him if you can come too?"

Ah, now there's an idea I like. "Yes. If he's going to get neighborly with my girl I think it is best that I be there as well."

Her cheeks flush. "Alright. I will ask him if you can come too."

Satisfied, I guide her out to the car waiting to take us to the park.

CHAPTER ELEVEN

CARI

Central Park is quite crowded already. With the clear blue sky, the sun happily beaming down, and the temperature hovering near eighty degrees, it really is a perfect day to be outdoors. Holding my hand, Deven leads me to a section of the park that is not as crowded.

"When I was younger, my father would bring me to work with him, and we would come here for lunch. He would tell me all sorts of stories. Some funny, some serious, and some with a moral to it."

"He sounds like a great guy."

"He is." Deven shares with me some of the memories he has with his father here, and asks me about my special memories with my grandparents. He listens intently as I tell him. The conversation eventually changes to the progress of the Los Angeles office. He updates me on the construction which is coming along as scheduled. He plans on deploying some of his human resources team out there in a few weeks to start recruiting. A few other members of the New York team will also be sent to L.A. to help get things set-up.

Every now and then, I can't help sneaking glances at the yummy eye candy beside me. Wearing a loose white button-down over a white T-shirt paired with khakis, he still manages to look hot. It's hard not to notice all the women turning their heads to admire him.

We wind up at the Loeb Boathouse where Deven rents a rowboat. I can barely take my eyes off of his flexing biceps each time he rows. He stops rowing when we are at an acceptable distance away from the other rowboats. I can't stop admiring the beautiful emerald green grass and trees skirting the glistening lake. "This is all so pretty to look at."

"Oh, I don't know about that. I think you're so much prettier to look at."

He looks at me adoringly and my cheeks become rosy. I avert my gaze to the water. "I don't think so," I whisper and bite down on my lower lip.

Deven leans forward and tips my chin up. With his eyes locked on mine, he gently tugs on my lower lip releasing it. "I disagree."

I've never had a guy compliment me as much as he does, but I've also never been with anyone like Deven. He is good to me, and he makes me feel beautiful, and safe. I don't have the fear that I usually have when a guy is interested in me.

He takes my hand in his. "I won't be around next week. I have to go away on business."

"Back to L.A.?"

He shakes his head. "No, this time it's Hong Kong." Oh. He'll be so far away. "It's kind of last minute, but this trip is important. If I can get a deal secured this time around it will open a lot of doors for BG."

"Part of your global expansion plan?"

"Yes, it is."

"I hope it goes well then. How long will you be gone?"

"Two weeks. I leave tomorrow morning."

"So soon?" Why does not seeing him for two weeks seem like eternity?

"I'm afraid so. I can't let the opportunity pass me by."

"Of course not. You must be earning a lot of frequent flyer miles with all the business trips you are taking."

"I'm trying to. I can use some free trips in the near future." He chuckles and picks up the oars to start rowing again.

CHAPTER TWELVE

DEVEN

Cari is much different than any one of the girls I have ever been with. It's a good different. Being with her is invigorating.

I wish we could stay here on the lake all afternoon, but I have a surprise waiting for her. What I have planned for her is something I've never done before. I grab the oars and start to row back. Once the boat has been returned, we walk around The Lake passing through Bethesda Terrace. I send a quick text to Mauricio from my phone to make sure he has everything ready.

"Are you hungry?"

"Yes." I love that she is not shy about her hunger.

"Good. I've got a perfect spot for us to have lunch." I take her soft delicate hand in mine and interlace my fingers with hers. I lead the way to Sheep Meadow where Mauricio is waiting. I see the blanket spread out with the picnic basket on top of it. Mauricio steps away as he sees us approach. She gasps.

"Our lunch?"

I nod and I'm rewarded with the most beautiful smile. I like making her happy. I've never had a picnic in the park before, but there's a romantic appeal to it. We sit down and I reach into the basket. I pull out the sandwiches and place them down on the blanket. Reaching back into the basket I take out two bottles of sparkling water, two containers of fruit salad, and a slice of cake. I look up at Cari and am mesmerized. She's extraordinarily beautiful. Her hair is slightly blowing in the wind, and she's sitting with her legs crossed in front of her completely at ease. How I wish I could kiss her now with abandon.

"What's the matter?" she asks when she catches me staring at her.

"Nothing." I shake my head. "Nothing at all."

She unwraps her sandwich and takes a bite of it. We talk and laugh while eating our lunch.

"That was the best mozzarella and prosciutto sandwich I've ever had." She crumbles up the wrapper and takes a drink from her bottle of water.

"Glad you liked it. I hope you saved room for dessert."

"Oh no. I don't think I have any room left."

"Not even for red velvet?"

Her eyes light up. "That's my favorite! How did you know?"

I shrug. "Lucky guess." Can't really go wrong with red velvet can I?

"In that case, I think I can make an exception."

"There's only one slice here. Do you mind if we share?"

"Not at all."

"Good." I remove the plastic wrapping from the spoon.

"Is there another spoon in the basket?"

I look in the basket and pretend to search for another spoon. I deliberately had Mauricio make sure only one spoon was packed. "I'm afraid not. Looks like we'll have to share a spoon as well."

"Oh." Is she repulsed by my suggestion?

"Let me feed the cake to you."

"Okay."

I cut off a small piece of cake with the spoon and feed it to her. Her eyelids flutter and her eyes close as she slowly chews the cake.

"Mmmm. This is delicious." Oh hell, I'm so turned on. I shift a little so that no evidence starts to surface. "May I return the favor and feed you?"

Holy shit. She wants to feed me? I never had a girl want to feed me. I immediately nod my head. This is a new experience. I open my mouth and she places the spoon into it. The cake is delicious, but the beauty in front of me is much more delicious.

"This is the first time I have ever been on a picnic. I like it."

"I'm glad. I have to admit it's my first time too."

"Thank you for such a wonderful day. Everything has been perfect." She leans forward and kisses my cheek. Her kiss is so sweet it warms me in a way I haven't felt before.

"Cari, you don't need to thank me." I tap her nose with my finger. "The day's not over yet." I take her hand and leave a kiss on the top of her hand.

We stay at the park a little while longer enjoying each other's company before finally departing, and going back to her apartment. I settle on the couch hoping she sits next to me, but she chooses to sit in the chair next to the couch instead.

"Come sit beside me." She moves to sit next to me on the couch.

I want to talk to her about taking the next step. I want nothing more than for her to be mine. I do not want to see her with any other guy especially her British neighbor. She has no inkling how beautiful she is, and how many men take notice of her.

I lean forward, elbows on my knees as I rub my hands together. "There's something I want to talk to you about."

"I'm all ears."

"The company does not have a non-fraternization policy in place, but I've always had this rule to not become involved with any of my employees." Her eyes widen in shock and her hand goes over her mouth. Shit. She's misinterpreting what I'm attempting to say. I reach for her hand. "No, it's not like that. The more time I spend with you, the more I want to be with you."

A look of comprehension washes over her face. "So you intend on breaking your own rule?"

Yeah, I'm breaking my rule, but I don't care anymore. After all, rules were made to be broken.

I look into her hypnotic jade eyes. "I already did the night I saw you at the club. I just didn't know it then." I sit back a little on the couch keeping her hand in mine. "From the first moment I laid eyes on you I was completely drawn to you. Cari, I want you, and I want you to be mine." She's looking back at me and her mouth is agape. I bring her hand to my heart and hold it there. "Say you'll be mine."

She doesn't respond immediately and looks to our entwined hands. Slowly her gaze meets mine. "You want an exclusive relationship? You and I?"

Christ. She's adorable. I smirk. "Yeah, that's how it's supposed to work."

"Yes. I want that too."

My heart swells enormously and I have the biggest, goofiest grin on my face.

"Are we keeping our relationship a secret?"

The office gossipmongers will have a field day if they discover our relationship. Cari doesn't need to be labeled or become the hot topic of their mindless conversations. "I don't let worthless gossip or people's opinion affect me, but I don't want to make it uncomfortable for you as you are around them a lot more than I am."

"What do you suggest?"

I pull her to me and kiss her hair. "We'll be discreet. We won't say anything just like the night we went out to Nobu. When we are in the office we will maintain our professional relationship in front of everyone."

"And outside of the office?"

"It's really no one's business except ours. When I return from Hong Kong, we are going to spend a lot more time together."

We continue to talk well into the night opting to take-in Chinese food for dinner. I want this sweet girl to be with me for as long as I can have her...forever if it's possible. She's everything I am looking for, and she's the first girl who isn't after me for my looks, my status, or my money. She's brought happiness back into my life and now it's my turn to make her happy just because she deserves it.

~ * ~

CARI

For so long there has been a void in my life, a hole in my heart. I avoided getting close to any guy, and then Deven waltzed into my life. Instantly he filled the void and made the aching pain in my heart stop.

Today has been the best day I have had in a long time. It's almost midnight, and Deven is getting ready to go so he can prepare for his overseas trip. He reaches for the doorknob and suddenly spins around facing me. His eyes are smoldering, and I swallow hard.

"Do you have any idea how beautiful you are Cari? Right now, I want nothing more than to kiss you before I leave."

"So what's stopping you?"

He closes the small distance between us, and cradles my face in his hands. My heart is pounding loud and fast. His lips brush against mine and that same tingling feeling I had the first time he kissed me reappears. The kiss is slow, tender, and long. With his hands still cradling my face, he pulls back to give us both some air, and gently rests his forehead against mine. He moves forward and pins me up against the wall.

"And this is so you don't forget me while I'm gone." His mouth comes crashing down on mine. This kiss is much more urgent, and fervent. His tongue finds mine and tangos with it. He slips an arm around my waist pressing our bodies together. I can feel his manhood pressed up against me. My body is on fire. I shove my hands into his hair and he lets out a moan.

"Cari," he says breathlessly. He plants a few kisses down my neck making me shiver.

I am no expert on kissing, but from my limited experience that was the best kiss I ever had. I never knew a kiss could be so good. Kissing him is heavenly. *He's heavenly.*

"I am going to miss you like crazy." He strokes my cheek with his thumb.

I look up at him through my long lashes. "Right back at you."

"There's a huge time difference between us, but I'll email you each day."

"Okay." I hug him tightly.

He places a kiss on the top of my head. "It's getting late. Get some rest. I'll email you when I get to Hong Kong."

"Alright. Have a safe trip."

He nods, and opens the door. "Dream of me."

"I will."

"Lock the door immediately."

"Okay." I love his concern for my safety.

After we say good bye, I lock the door behind him. Leaning against the door, I close my eyes running my fingers along my lips remembering the taste of him. Feeling his hardness awakened a desire in me which had lain dormant for years. What the heck is Deven Blake doing to me?

CHAPTER THIRTEEN

July

DEVEN

The trip to Hong Kong was an exhausting one. Thunderstorms had started to move into the New York metro area close to our departure time resulting in our flight being delayed by a few hours. I brought Mayleen with me on this trip since school was out for the summer. The last time I traveled to Hong Kong she could not go due to a conflict with school and sports. My sister is fascinated with the Asian culture as she should be.

May is ecstatic to go on her first trip to Hong Kong. She talked my ear off most of the trip. My garrulous sister caught me up on all the gossip at her school. I don't normally sleep much on the plane, but on this particular flight I wish sleep did not elude me so I did not have to listen to gossip.

After arriving and collecting our bags, our hired car drives us to the Shangri-La Hotel where we will be staying the next couple of weeks. We have a two-bedroom suite overlooking Victoria Harbour.

"This is so awesome! All my girlfriends are going to be so jealous when I post this on Facebook!"

"We've stayed in rooms just as nice as this with mom and dad. And I'm sure your girlfriends have stayed in rooms like this."

"Some, but not all."

"May, sometimes you are just as arrogant as they are." I playfully ruffle her hair.

"Hey, I resent that! I am nothing like them."

I chuckle. "I beg to differ."

She pouts. "Some brother you are."

"I prefer if you not be a hypocrite, or a snob. You should not talk shit about them and then do it yourself."

She sighs very loudly and grabs her bags. "I think I'll go to my room now."

"There are two bedrooms here. Choose the one you want."

She takes a peek into each room and lets me know which room she selects. I go to my room and unpack my suitcase. After I am done unpacking I open up my laptop and send a short email to Cari. The memory of kissing Cari is still vivid in my mind. Kissing her was fucking unbelievable. If it weren't for this trip I would have stayed and kissed her all night long. I go through the rest of my emails, and then go to May's room to ask if she wants to do a little exploring and grab something to eat.

"May, do you –" May is sound asleep on the bed. Looks like jetlag has hit her. There's no doubt the long flight and all that chattering she did wore her down. I search the closet for an extra blanket and cover her with it. I move into the parlor to watch TV before slowly drifting to sleep.

~ * ~

On our first full day in Hong Kong, I take May to Jumbo Kingdom for dim sum. This infamous floating restaurant sits in the Aberdeen Harbour, and is often busy but I know May will enjoy the experience more than the food. The restaurant is packed, but fortunately for us we don't have to wait too long to be seated. Throughout our meal, May tells me which shopping malls she wants to go to. *Can someone please shoot me?* The shopping here is great, but I did not bring her along so she can spend her time and money buying things for herself and her friends.

Since I have a free day today, I planned out our day accordingly. After dim sum, we visited The Peak. As we rode the tram up it was amusing to see the expression on May's face. She looked frightened as she held onto my arm the entire trip both ways. She had no faith that the tram would make it up and down safely. When we got to the top she was not as enthralled with the stunning view of Hong Kong's skyline like I was. I was going to suggest some more sightseeing; however, May was persistent on going shopping so I conceded.

"I had so much fun today!" May says as we place the shopping bags down in the parlor. "I can't wait to do some more shopping tomorrow. I want a new Chanel bag."

"You still have room on your card?"

"I most definitely do."

I roll my eyes. "Well, remember we still have to go through customs."

"I know. Mom warned me that I have to watch how much I buy."

"Alright then. I'm going to check my emails and do some work."

"Sure, *di gor*."

May just called me her "big brother" in Cantonese. "When did you learn that?"

"Today. Google translation is great."

I laugh. "Very good."

"I'm going to go post some stuff on Facebook, and then can we go to dinner once you're done?"

"Yes."

Spending quality time with May has been real nice. We haven't done much together since I took over for Dad. My free time was spent either visiting Dad or working. And with Dad not home anymore I need to be around for May more than ever.

CHAPTER FOURTEEN

CARI

The entire week had crawled. I'm removing my clothes out of the washer and throwing them into the dryer when I hear someone call my name. I look up and see Zach leaning against the table next to me.

"Hi, Zach."

"Hello. What a lovely surprise to see a beautiful lady in the laundry room."

I flush.

"Laundry day for you?"

"Yeah." I eye his laundry bag. "And for you as well?"

"Yeah. It's rare I do my own laundry, but I have some time off so I thought I would do it myself instead of sending it out."

He sends his laundry out? I throw the last article of clothing in the dryer and start it. Zach separates his laundry into two machines. All the whites in one machine, and all the colored clothing in the other.

"Where's your roomie?"

"He's out with his boyfriend."

"No plans with your boyfriend today?"

I shake my head. "He's in Hong Kong on a business trip."

He stops what he's doing and looks at me. "What does he do for a living?"

"He's the CEO of the Blake Group."

"The Blake Group? That name sounds quite familiar. Wait. Don't they have a lot of property in Manhattan?"

"Yes, they do. And they keep adding more to their portfolio."

"Hence the trip to Hong Kong."

"Yes."

"Hong Kong is amazing. The country, the people, the food are all phenomenal. And fabulous shopping."

"I'm not really into shopping, but I would like to go there someday."

He smiles and returns to his task of adding the detergent into the machine. He has a great physique like Deven, but Deven is much hotter. He turns around before I have a chance to look away and catches me gawking at him. My cheeks heat up again.

He smiles and pretends he didn't see me staring at him. "What is on your agenda today?"

"I don't have any plans."

"Why don't you come over for lunch? I make a delicious tuna niçoise salad."

Lunch. Alone in his apartment. Deven does not want me alone with him, and since we just became exclusive I'm not going to go against his request.

"Maybe we can go to a restaurant instead," he says scratching the back of his head when I take too long to answer.

Yes, being in public would be much better.

"A restaurant is good."

He pulls out his cell from his pocket. "How does one o'clock sound?"

"One sounds perfect."

"Great. Come and get me when you're ready then." He winks at me and I hurry out of the laundry room before he sees my flushed face again.

~ * ~

I show up at Zach's apartment a little after our agreed upon time. The sky is dark and it looks like it's going to rain soon. I have my rain boots on, and bring along an umbrella with me. We head to the nearby sandwich shop just a block and a half away. Just as I'm about to take a bite out of my sandwich my text message alert goes off. I check my phone and see that it's a message from Deven.

D: I miss you.

My heart melts. I type back my response.

Me: I miss you too.

I place my phone back down and bite into my sandwich.

"That's a big smile on your face. Your boyfriend?"

"Yeah."

"How long have you two been seeing each other?"

"Very recently."

"He's a lucky guy to have such a pretty girl."

I don't know why, but compliments just make me blush. I wish I can turn the blushing off. He's nice enough to change the subject and tells me what he does for a living. I learn he's a model and he has appeared on several magazine covers and is often traveling for his job. He's back for a few days before he has to go abroad again for some more shoots. He asks me about my job and I tell him what I do. I notice the surprise on his face when he realizes I work for Deven's company. I should have explained to him how Deven and I first met, but I don't. Sadly, he tells me how he had his heart broken when he was living in England. Six months before he was to marry he caught his fiancée cheating on him with his best friend. Being blindsided by the person you care about really stinks.

CHAPTER FIFTEEN

DEVEN

The remainder of the time in Hong Kong passes by quickly between business meetings, a little bit of sightseeing that I managed to convince May to do, and of course more shopping. With each passing day I become more and more anxious to fly home so I can be with Cari again.

May and I arrive at the airport a little early so she can do a little more shopping. My sister is a shopaholic, and I think she cleaned out all of the designer stores in Hong Kong. I finally put an end to her shopping spree when I declare my hunger. I want to eat before boarding the plane.

"Deven, who did you buy the Gucci scarf and bag for?"

Shit. I forgot how nosey she can be. I keep chewing so I can prolong having to answer her question. She puts down her chopsticks and waves her hand in front of my face.

"Tell me Deven."

"It's for someone."

"Who? A girl?"

"A friend."

She squints her eyes at me.

I lay my chopsticks over my bowl. "What?"

"Do you always buy your friends such expensive gifts?"

I raise my eyebrows. She bought her best friend a Fendi bag, and she's questioning me?

"Are you being a hypocrite?"

"Are you keeping a secret from me?"

May is so persistent.

"Fine. It's for my girlfriend."

She squeals in delight drawing attention to our table.

"I'm sorry. I am just so happy for you."

She may be persistent, but she can also be very sweet. I can't help but smile widely. "I'm happy too."

"Who is she? When are you going to bring her over so I can meet her? Where did you meet her?"

"Whoa. Too many questions at once."

"No, it's not. Start by telling me what her name is."

"Her name is Carilyn, but she likes to be called Cari. And I met her at a club."

"When do I get to meet her?"

"Soon."

"How soon?"

"Soon, but there's something you should know."

"What's that?"

"She works at BG."

"Holy shit!"

I scowl at her. "Mayleen Blake, that is unacceptable language."

"Oh, please. Is she your assistant?"

"No. She works for Myra."

"Doesn't Myra have a reputation?"

"Unfortunately, but I had a talk with her." I tell her about what Myra did to Cari, and the ultimatum I gave her.

"My friends are going to be so jealous when I tell them you are taken."

"My personal life is none of their business."

She rolls her eyes.

Cari became the subject of our conversation up until we boarded the plane. I was thankful she chose to watch a movie and go to sleep on the flight back to New York. I can hardly wait to get back home and see my beautiful girl again.

CHAPTER SIXTEEN

CARI

The two weeks without Deven had been long. I had been looking forward to seeing Deven when he returned to the office on Monday, but it never happened. It was impossible to see him during the work week. His calendar was filled with outside appointments and meetings Catrina had set up for him prior to his trip. And the days he did come into the office, he came in very early and left very late. It became easier to talk and exchange text messages during the week instead. He promised we would spend Saturday together.

I have never spent more than two minutes picking out an outfit. I want to look pretty and sexy for Deven so I finally pick out a low-cut tank top with short shorts. I'm pulling my hair up into a ponytail when I hear whistling. Rodrigo is leaning against the door frame wearing his polka dot pajamas and a bandana around his head.

"Wow Cari! You could give a gay man a hard on."

I giggle. "Too revealing?"

He shakes his head. "No, it's perfect. You look sexy honey. Are you looking to get some tonight from your man?"

My eyes widen and I feel the heat rise in my cheeks. "Rodrigo!"

"He's not going to be able to resist you once he sees you."

"That's the plan."

Rodrigo gasps. "Carilyn Jade Snow! You always seem to surprise me."

"I really like him Rodrigo. I just want to make sure he notices me, that's all."

"Honey, he *will* notice you."

Uh-oh. Rodrigo has that stern look on his face. The look an older brother gives his younger sister when she is about to go out on a date.

"What is it Rodrigo?"

"You know I want nothing more than for you to be happy…"

Here we go. "There's a but to this."

He crosses his arms. "Be careful, okay? I don't want to see anything happen to you again."

"I will. Deven's different though."

Rodrigo comes over to give me a big bear hug. "I hope so."

"You'll see for yourself when you meet him."

"Okay. Love you."

"Love you too. You should change your clothes before he gets here."

"Why? I'm comfortable."

I plead with him. "Please." Rodrigo rolls his eyes and heads to his room to change out of his pajamas.

Twenty minutes later and punctual as usual, the intercom buzzer goes off. Rodrigo buzzes him in and looks at me. "You ready?"

"As ever."

I'm nervous about the initial meeting between Deven and Rodrigo. Rodrigo has always been protective of me especially after what happened with my ex-boyfriend. It is very important to me that they get along. Rodrigo smiles and opens the door for Deven.

"Hey Deven. I'm Rodrigo." He extends his hand.

"It's a pleasure to finally meet you Rodrigo. I've heard a lot of good things about you." Deven shakes his hand. He does not seem uncomfortable around Rodrigo and a wave of relief washes over me. My last boyfriend was a homophobic and he was immediately uncomfortable being near Rodrigo.

"Please come in." Rodrigo moves to the side and lets him in.

My heart does that fluttery thing as soon as I see him. "Hi Deven."

Deven puts down the bag he has in his hand. Bridging the gap between us, he wraps his arms around me, and lifts me off the ground. He smacks a kiss on my lips. "You look so sexy," he says placing a kiss on my cheek before putting me down. He smells like fresh linen.

"She always does," Rodrigo mutters as he saunters past us to take a seat in the oversized chair in the living room.

Deven reaches for the bag on the floor and snags my hand pulling me down next to him on the couch.

Rodrigo sits tall, crosses his legs, and focuses on Deven. "Isn't it something that Cari works for you?"

I scowl at him. "Rodrigo."

He waves his hand in the air and pats Deven's knee. I sit there with my mouth agape. *What is he doing?* I close my mouth and turn back at Deven to make sure he is not feeling awkward, but he doesn't appear to be bothered by Rodrigo patting his knee.

"I like to think fate brought us together." Deven flashes his sexy dimpled smile.

"Maybe it did."

"Cari, I have something for you that I picked up while I was in Hong Kong. I apologize Rodrigo I don't have anything for you, but I'd like to have you join us for dinner one night," he says as he puts the shopping bag on the coffee table. I see the bag, and so does Rodrigo. Gucci.

"How nice of you to offer. Dinner sounds good. Can I invite my partner?"

"Absolutely."

Rodrigo smiles and I can tell he's not going to have a problem with Deven.

"Open it Cari. I want to see what you got," Rodrigo says.

I take out the small flat box first and lift the top off.

"Oh, my! This is beautiful," I say as I take the scarf out of the box and run my fingers through the silky material.

"Good taste," Rodrigo adds.

I remove the bigger box from the bag. I open the box to see a Gucci leather tote bag.

"Thank you Deven, but this is too much. I can't accept this."

"Of course you can. You deserve only the finest." He makes me feel so special like I am his treasure.

"You sure do sweetie. Besides, he won't be returning that," Rodrigo adds.

I look back at Deven. "Thank you so much. They're beautiful presents and so thoughtful of you." I hug him and place the items back into their respective boxes.

"Cari mentioned your company is opening an office in L.A," Rodrigo says to Deven.

"Yes, we are."

"I love L.A. I haven't been there in years, but I would love to go back."

"When was the last time you were there?"

"About ten years ago."

"I'd love to go too someday," I chime in.

"I can arrange that." Deven smirks. Of course he can.

"She needs to get away. Maybe you'll be the one who can convince her to." *Sheesh, thanks Rodrigo.*

"I can be very convincing," he says taking my hand and lifting it to his mouth.

"Have you bumped into any celebrities in L.A.?"

Deven turns to Rodrigo. "Yes, I have. I know a few of them too."

"Really? Who do you hobnob with?"

Deven tells Rodrigo, and Rodrigo starts bombarding him with questions about those celebrities. I am not into celebrity gossip or their lifestyle like Rodrigo is. I watch and listen as the two of them jump from one topic to another. They chat like they are old friends catching up on lost years. And that's my sign that Rodrigo approves of him.

~ * ~

DEVEN

I like Rodrigo. He is friendly and is protective of Cari. It's comforting to know when I am not with Cari he will take care of her. Rodrigo and I are alone while Cari gets her handbag from her room.

"Cari is like a sister to me. She's been through a lot in her life, and I'm the closest thing she has to a family."

"I know. She told me, and I'm glad she has you."

"She's a good person."

"I know that too."

"I want her to be happy, and she deserves to be happy."

"I'm devoted to making her happy. She means a lot to me."

He put his palm up. "She means a lot to me too, but you don't know her like I do." There's something more to what he just said.

"I know enough about her to want to pursue a relationship with her. I don't need to explain how I feel about her to you, but I do care a lot about Cari."

He stares at me uncertain if I meant what I just said. "Very well then," he says accepting what I told him.

"Are you ready to go Deven?" Cari asks when she comes back into the living room.

"I am." I stand up, and so does Rodrigo. "It was nice to meet you, and we'll have that dinner soon."

"Sounds good."

I walk behind Cari and place my hand on the small of her back.

"Wait Cari!" Rodrigo says just as she is about to open the door. He runs down the hall and returns with something in his hands. He shoves it into Cari's hands. "Just in case."

I look to see what it is. It's a couple of foil packages. I can't help the grin that appears on my face. Cari's cheeks are flushed and she quickly stashes the packets in her handbag. She hurries to the elevator and I keep pace with her.

Holding her hand in mine I lead the way to my car which is three short blocks away. She is turning men's heads as we walk down the street, and I don't like it. I know I have a beautiful woman with me, but they should keep their eyes off of her. I stop and she stops with me. I take her other hand. She looks up at me. God damn, she's fucking beautiful.

"You're turning men's heads."

"I am? I don't mean to."

I pull her into a tight embrace. I love the feel of her in my arms. "I know. You're mine Cari." She nods her head. I take out my key remote and the doors unlock. Cari's eyes widen as she takes in my black Porsche Cayenne Turbo.

"This is yours? You drive?"

Her expression made me laugh. "Yeah. I do know how to drive."

Her cheeks turn pink. "Um, nice car."

"Thank you. It's one of my favorites."

I open the passenger door for her to get in. I close the door after her and walk around to the driver's side.

"One of your favorites?"

"Yes."

"What are your other favorites?"

"Jaguar, and Maserati."

"Do you have one of each?"

"I don't have a Maserati yet." I wink at her. Her mouth drops open. "Ready?"

"Yes. Where are we going?"

"It's a surprise." I smile and pull the car onto the road.

CHAPTER SEVENTEEN

DEVEN

"Where are we?" She asks observing the grounds as she gets out of the car.

"We are at Gillette Castle."

She glances at the stone building. "How about that? A castle in the woods."

I brief her on the history of the castle on our way to the ticket window. I pay for our admission, and we are admitted inside William Gillette's former home. There is a tour that we initially join but then separate to explore the rest of the castle and grounds on our own. We stroll through the grounds and stop at the bridge.

"It's so peaceful here. I understand why he chose to live out here."

"It is peaceful."

There's a stretch of silence between us.

"Cari, there's something I want to ask you…something personal."

She looks at me with questioning eyes. "What is it?"

"How did your mother die?"

She crosses her arms, and her eyes fixate on the lily pond.

"You don't have to tell me if it's too painful to talk about," I say softly.

"I don't have any memories of her. I've only seen her in pictures. She was very pretty, but Grams said she was a very spontaneous person. During high school she had a huge crush on some guy. He asked her out, and on their first and only date, I was conceived. My grandparents told me my father did not want anyone to know she was pregnant. He wanted her to have an abortion, but my mother refused." That's the problem with us men. We have a hard time keeping our dicks in our pants and it can get us into trouble.

"And because she refused, he did not want anything to do with her. After I was born my mother couldn't care for me, and she suffered a mental breakdown. My grandmother was so busy caring for me she couldn't tend to my mother. Grams didn't deliberately do it. She just couldn't handle both of us. My grandfather tried to get help for my mother but she was unresponsive to him. Then one morning, my grandparents received a call that she had been in a fatal car accident, and they never forgave themselves for her death."

How horrible for her to have lost her mother like that. I instantly put my arms around her and pull her close to me. She uncrosses her arms and wraps them around my waist pressing her cheek to my chest. I close my eyes and lay my cheek on top of her head.

"I'm so sorry," I whisper holding her tightly. "Are you curious to know who your father is?"

She pulls away and shakes her head. "No. If he wanted to claim me as his daughter he would have made every effort to find me, but he never did. He got scared and ran. My grandparents never wanted me to know him. They considered him to be dead too since he did not want me." She shrugs. "There was a brief time when I was younger and I wanted to know who he was. I used to hope he would surprise me one day and tell me how much he missed me and loved me, and wanted me. But it never happened."

Her father is a douche. She's better off not knowing him. He does not deserve a place in her life.

"I really like it here." She changes the topic and that's my cue not to pry anymore.

"Let's take a walk." I wrap my arm around her waist and guide her into the woods. I take her deeper into the woods away from the castle so we can be alone.

"Are we lost Deven?"

"No. I just want to be alone with you for a little while." I want to take her to a secluded spot so I can kiss her madly. She's trembling on this hot day, and I suspect it's not because she thinks we're lost. Does she think I'm going to hurt her?

"In the middle of the woods?" She has an alarmed expression, and her voice has a slight quiver to it. She's definitely frightened, but why?

"You're terrified." Her gaze falls to the ground. "Look at me." She looks up at me, and there's fear in her eyes. "I promise you I know where we are. We can go back if you feel uncomfortable."

"Yes, please. I want to go back."

"Okay." Still clasping her hand in mine we walk back in silence to the parking lot.

"Do you want to talk about what had you scared back there?"

"Not really."

"Alright. If and when you are ready to talk about it, I'll be here to listen. Whatever it is, I will protect you from it. I will never let anything happen to you."

I start the car and leave the parking lot. I keep her hand in mine as I drive. She's been quiet since the incident in the woods. "You okay?"

"Yeah."

"I'd like to take you back to my place, but only if you feel up to it."

"I want to go to your place."

"You do?"

Her beautiful smile appears. "I do."

CHAPTER EIGHTEEN

CARI

I breathe a deep sigh of relief when Deven did not pressure me to tell him why I wanted to leave the woods. He can't know. He can never know the reason why I freaked out in the woods. I do what I need to do to move past it and forget about it.

I'm stoked to be going to Deven's home. He pulls into a circular driveway under two tall glass towers. An illuminated glass fixture with the words "La Maison" etched in it sits in front of the driveway and is surrounded by a beautiful waterfall.

"Good afternoon, Mr. Blake. Ma'am." A uniformed man approaches Deven, and gives us both a nod. He must be the valet.

"Good afternoon, Larry."

The valet gets into Deven's car and drives off to park it. The doorman opens the door for us and I follow Deven into the lobby. Holy moly! The lobby is spacious and elegant with its marble floors, light wood panels, and sleek and modern furniture. A huge glass chandelier is suspended high above the center of the lobby. There is a separate sitting room with a fireplace.

"Good afternoon, Mr. Blake." The concierge behind the large granite desk smiles and bats her eyes at Deven. Isn't she a little too old for him? Like all his other female admirers her smile fades as soon as I come into view.

"Good afternoon, Bianca," Deven responds, and continues to lead me through the lobby towards the elevator.

"Nice lobby," I murmur as he presses the button for the elevator.

He shrugs. "It's alright. The complex also has an on outdoor terrace with a retractable roof, a fitness center, and a pool." This is what money gets you.

The doors to the elevator open and we step in. He punches a few numbers into a keypad and then presses the button for the thirty-eighth floor. He leans back and tilts his head up to look at the digital display. The letters "PH" display and the doors open. Holy crap! He lives in the penthouse. He guides me out into a private foyer. There are two doors side by side, and on the wall next to one of the doors is a biometric machine. He punches in another code, and places his finger on the glass window next to the keypad. There's a clicking sound and he opens the door allowing me to enter first. I walk into the vestibule which leads to a corridor.

He shuts the door behind him. "Come, I'd like to show you around." He turns to his right and brings me to the end of the corridor. The living room is to the left, and his personal gym is the room to the right. There is an abundance of natural lighting streaming through his floor to ceiling windows. He has an unobstructed view of Westchester. His living room is three times the size of my living room. It's beautifully furnished. There are three couches and a coffee table that sit on top of an area rug which lies over the rosewood floor. A large HDTV hangs above his gas fireplace. Along another wall is a wall unit stocked with books, photos, and some antiques.

"Let me show you the other side."

I follow him back into the hallway. We pass by a couple of doors on our right where two spare bedrooms are. He opens a door and we continue down the hallway to the other side of the penthouse. His home office is here. It's a replica of his Manhattan office complete with floor to ceiling windows, and a private bathroom. At the end of the hall is the enormous master suite. His mahogany king size bed and its leather headboard is in the center of the room flanked by matching nightstands. Off to the side is a smaller room separated by sliding French doors. In the room is a leather chair and ottoman, a round glass table, a gas fireplace, and shelves and shelves full of books.

"This is my reading room."

"I could lose myself in this room with all these books."

He chuckles. "My little bookworm."

I smile back at him loving his pet name for me.

"I think you may like the next room just as much if not more."

"Is that so?"

"Come see for yourself." He leads me back into the bedroom and slides open another door. My eyes expand, and I cannot keep my mouth from dropping open. I step into the commodious and luxurious marble bathroom. If Rodrigo saw this he would be in heaven. A huge Roman tub and shower stall occupy one side of the bathroom. On the opposite side are two separate sinks, and two separate rooms for the commodes. Why does he need two of each? One for him and one for his lover? A pang of jealousy hits me as I think about one of his lovers being here. I frown, and shake off the thought. He's with me now, and that's what matters.

"Is something wrong?"

"Um, no. Why?"

"You had a frown on your face a second ago."

I need to do a better job of hiding my expressions. "I was just thinking how much Rodrigo would love a bathroom like this. It's so roomy."

He rubs the back of his neck and looks embarrassed. "Yeah, I, uh, like a lot of space."

"I can see that." There are no curtains or shades for the windows. "Are you not concerned about your privacy when you're bathing?"

"I don't think anyone can really see this high up." He walks over to a panel and presses a button. "Look," he says pointing to the windows which are now opaque. How cool is that? "I'm not one for public indecency. At the touch of this button here, the windows will fog up offering privacy. As a matter of fact, all of my windows have the capability to become private with a touch of a button." Sheesh! Having money has no limits.

"Your bachelor pad is impressive."

He grins. "Thank you. I originally wanted the penthouse upstairs, but it was already purchased by the time I made my offer so I had to settle for second best. At least I still have the entire floor."

This is second best? I can't even imagine what the penthouse upstairs is like.

"Your place is so clean. Do you really live here?"

He chuckles. "I have my housekeeper to thank for maintaining my tidy home."

"Your housekeeper comes every day to clean?"

"Pretty much except on the weekends unless I request for her to come. Would you like something to drink? A glass of wine?"

"Do you have water?"

"I do. Spring or sparkling?"

"Sparkling is fine."

"Let's visit my favorite room in the house then."

CHAPTER NINETEEN

DEVEN

Asking Cari to come back to my penthouse is a monumental step for me. I have never brought a girl to my home, but I wanted Cari here. I am not the type to bring any girl back to my place, but Cari is special. My home and my privacy are utmost important to me. It's one of the reasons why I live in a secure building. One-nighters used to happen at the girl's place. Never in my home. But with Cari, all the rules change. I want her to feel comfortable being here because I want her to start staying here with me.

I bring her into my gourmet kitchen equipped with top-of-the-line stainless steel appliances. I open the refrigerator and grab a large bottle of Pellegrino, and two glasses from one of the cabinets. I pour the water into the glasses and hand one to her.

"Cheers," I say and raise my glass to hers.

"Cheers."

We both drink from our glasses. I place my glass on the marble countertop and then take the glass from her hand and set it down next to mine. I inch closer to her and caress her cheek with my knuckles. She stares back at me with hungry eyes making my heart pound frenziedly. Our lips come together, and our teeth clash as our kiss becomes desperate. My hands glide down her body while her hands glide down my back stopping on my ass and giving it a squeeze. Holy fuck!

Once we pull apart, I ask her to stay for dinner and she agrees. "Let me see what I have in the refrigerator."

"You can cook?"

"I can indeed. I can cook, and I can drive. Does that turn you on?" I wiggle my eyebrows and it makes her laugh. Her laugh is infectious.

She throws her hair behind her shoulder. "So what's on the menu tonight?"

I open my commercial grade Sub-Zero refrigerator and peer into it. Shit. My housekeeper did not do any grocery shopping. "It seems that my housekeeper did not stock up my refrigerator." As much as I rather stay in and do nothing but kiss her, we have to eat. "There's a good Thai restaurant nearby we can go to."

"I love Thai food."

"I know." I remember everything she tells me.

"I don't think I am dressed appropriately to go out for dinner," she says looking down at her outfit.

"We can always take something in instead." I circle my arms around her waist and press her tightly to me. "But if you rather eat out, your attire is fine."

"Do you think maybe I can borrow a sweater or something?"

"Anything you want."

"Thank you." Her hands come around my face pulling it down to hers. She teases my bottom lip with her teeth and then licks it. Fuck me. That is hot. My hands cup her ass and I lift her up onto the counter. She wraps her legs around my waist, and pulls me in for a zealous kiss. I'm aching for her. I want to sweep her up into my arms and take her back to my bedroom, but I refrain. I don't want to rush her into anything especially after how frightened she was earlier. I just need to keep my pants zipped up until the time is right.

CHAPTER TWENTY

August

CARI

The company's outing to Dorney Park has me at the office three hours earlier than usual. The charter buses are parked in front of BG ready for the employees to board and depart at a quarter to seven. I wait for Alana, and Jeremy in the lobby. Groups of people have already started to gather outside of the building conversing while waiting to board the bus.

"Hey gorgeous," Jeremy says leaning in to hug me.

"Hey Jeremy."

"I love the company outings. No work, and all play."

"Hello, hello!" Alana comes towards us and gives us a hug and an air kiss. "I am so excited. Cari, you must sit next to me on the bus so we can talk."

"How do you know Cari wants to sit next to you? Maybe she wants to sit next to me." Jeremy puts his arms around my shoulders.

"But I want to tell her about my wedding plans."

I interrupt them. "I think I should have a say on who I get to sit next to."

"I agree." The three of us turn around to find Deven standing there with his hands on his hips. He has on an Under Armour t-shirt and shorts. *Drool. He looks yummy.* His eyes narrow when he sees Jeremy's arm around me.

"Good morning, Deven," Alana says first.

"Good morning, sir," Jeremy says.

"Good morning," I say softly.

"Good morning everyone. Jeremy, please take your arm off of Miss Snow."

"Yes, sir." Jeremy does as he is told.

"Cari, did you decide who you will sit next to?" Deven asks.

"Umm...I'm still deciding."

"Why don't you remain neutral and sit next to me? Then they can sit next to each other."

Alana and Jeremy look at each other, and then back at Deven and I.

"Cari, you can sit next to Deven and we'll sit together," Alana offers pointing to her and Jeremy.

"Problem solved." Deven grins. He's happy he got his way. And so am I. I would not have been comfortable if one of the office girls ended up sitting next to him.

"Good morning everyone," says Lilah as she approaches us. Lilah is one of the pretty HR Managers at BG. She has long jet black hair, and a tendency to dress in tight clothing. And her attire today can attest to it. She has on teeny tiny shorts, and a loose white tank top that barely covers her breasts which are about to pop out of the bikini top she has on underneath. "Deven, I need to speak with you to go over some of the items before we start boarding."

"Sure." He glances at Alana, and Jeremy, but his gaze lingers on my face. "If you will all pardon me. Cari, I'll see you on bus number one." He goes to meet with Lilah. I watch Deven, but he does not stare at her like the other guys do.

"Ick! Can you believe what Lilah is wearing?" Alana looks repulsed.

"She's got some nice knockers."

"Jeremy!" Alana and I both say at the same time.

At a quarter to seven, Lilah announces everyone should start boarding. Alana, Jeremy, and I make our way to our designated bus.

"Sit anywhere you'd like," Lilah says from the first row.

I don't recognize anyone on the bus. I move up the aisle when I hear

Deven call my name. I turn my head and see him gesturing with his head to go back to the front. Deven says something to Lilah and I see her get up and move to the opposite side behind the driver's seat. I take the window seat and Deven settles down beside me. Once the buses are loaded, Deven gives the okay for the buses to depart.

After a few hours on the bus to Dorney Park we finally arrive. Lilah quickly reviews the rules again before letting everyone disperse into the park. Deven pulls me to the side.

"Jeremy needs to keep his hands off of you or he will find himself sitting in the unemployment office."

"You don't need to worry about him. I'm yours."

"Damn straight."

"Let's go Cari," Alana calls out to me.

Deven mentioned the other night he had no intention of going on any of the rides. A manager needed to be present in the designated picnic area in the event an employee needs assistance. He thought it would be best if he be the point person this year so everyone can have fun.

"Go enjoy yourself Cari. See you later," Deven says.

"Alright. See you later then." I jog over to Alana, and Jeremy.

"It figures Lilah would stay with Deven. I can't stand her," Alana mutters as we walk further away from Lilah, and Deven. "She and Myra should keep each other company."

"Misery keeping misery company." Jeremy laughs. "That's good!"

"Why don't you like Lilah?" I ask Alana.

"She's a fake, a kiss ass, and an all-around major bitch. Her ego is as big as her boobs. She tried to get me fired for insubordination because I did not acknowledge her in the elevator. Who does that?"

"Really?"

"Yeah. The Director of Human Resources at that time laughed it off."

"I think it's you Alana. She's never been like that towards anyone else," Jeremy says.

"I've never done anything to her. It's her big ego. And I see she's still after Deven."

Deven? Did she have a thing for him? "What do you mean?"

"They used to date. Did you see the smile on her face when you walked away from Deven? She's probably getting her claws on him now. I don't know what Deven ever saw in her in the first place," Alana says with a snort.

They used to date? My heart plunges to the ground as I absorb this startling information. Why didn't Deven mention this to me?

"How do you know they used to date?" I finally manage to ask.

"I overheard Lilah tell someone. At first, I thought she was lying, but my curiosity got the best of me and I did some research."

"Research?"

"Google, honey. You can get info on anyone. They both went to the same college and there was a picture of the two of them sitting on a lawn looking mighty cozy with each other."

I feel the color drain from my face. I don't want to hear anymore.

"Cari, are you feeling alright?"

I shake my head.

"You don't look too good. Sit down Cari," Jeremy says grasping my arm and guiding me over to a bench.

I mumble an excuse about breakfast not agreeing with me, and urge them to go on without me, but they refuse to leave me alone. Jeremy bought a bottle of ice cold water for me to drink. It made me feel a little better, but I don't want to sit here all day and ruin the fun for them. They have been looking forward to this day. After a few more minutes I force myself to enjoy the day with them.

I do end up having a great time with Alana, and Jeremy. When the time comes to board the bus back to Manhattan, I attempt to board the other bus with Alana, and Jeremy. I don't want to be on the same bus with Deven, and Lilah. I almost get away with it until Deven announces we all must board the same bus we came on.

Once Deven and his HR team accounted for everyone, the buses leave. I avoid Deven and listen to my playlist on my iPhone, but I can feel Deven's eyes on me. He gently pulls the earpod out of my ear.

"Did you have a good time today?"

I nod, and put my earpod back in my ear. He pulls my earpod out again. "Is something the matter?"

"No." *I'm such a bad liar.*

His eyes narrow with concern. "Are you sure?"

I repeat the process by taking back my earbud and putting it back in my ear giving him a nod while doing so. I close my eyes to evade any conversation with him on the trip back. My therapist once told me I need to confront the issues and stop burying them, but I'm not a confrontational person. How am I going to bring it up that I feel hurt and betrayed he kept his past relationship with Lilah from me?

"Cari." I slowly wake up from the nap I took on the way back, and see Deven's handsome face in front of mine. I rub my eyes and sit up looking ahead.

"We're back. Don't go far after the buses unload. Wait for me," Deven whispers.

I scurry off the bus and look for Alana, and Jeremy.

"Hey, we're going for drinks. Wanna come with us?" Alana asks.

"Another time. I think I'm going to go home and hit the sack early. Thanks for the invite."

"Anytime sweetie," Alana says.

We say our goodbyes. I search for Deven in the throngs of people on the sidewalk, but I don't see him. After a hot day in the sun, I feel drained and just want to go home, shower, and sleep. I walk to the subway station and head home.

CHAPTER TWENTY-ONE

DEVEN

Lilah has been talking non-stop to me since we got off the bus. She's mumbling something about the holiday party which is the company's next big event. Seeing that it's only August, I do not need to get involved until late October. It's a discussion that we can have later. I don't want to keep Cari waiting so I cut the conversation short. I look for Cari and can't seem to find her. I call her iPhone, but it goes straight to her voicemail. She probably got tired of waiting and went home. I hail a cab to Cari's place.

En route to her apartment, I keep trying to call her, but she doesn't answer. I buzz her apartment. No answer. What the fuck? Where she is? She seemed to be a little off on the way back though she claimed nothing was wrong. I hope she's okay. I lean against the wall of her building checking my emails.

Twenty minutes have passed, and I still can't get a hold of her. I'm just about to give up when I see her approaching. She sees me and stops.

"You left," I say to her.

She shrugs. "I didn't feel like hanging around."

"But I told you to wait for me. What's going on angel?"

"Nothing. I just have a headache."

"You should have told me. I would have accompanied you home."

She stares at the concrete sidewalk. Something is going on and it's not the headache. "Something is bothering you, and I want to know what it is."

When she looks back at me her eyes are misty. "I need to ask you something and I want you to give me an honest answer."

Honest answer? What the hell is this about? "I have been nothing but honest with you. What do you want to ask?"

"Why didn't you tell me you used to date Lilah?"

Shit.

"How did you know?"

"Google."

I squeeze at the tension building in the back of my neck. "We dated for a short time when we were in college, but it's been over for quite some time." Dating Lilah was the biggest mistake I made while attending college.

Her face softens a bit. "That explains why she seemed to be annoyed at me."

"When was this?"

"Today on the bus when you asked her to move."

I shrug. "I did not want to sit next to her. It's you who I wanted to sit next to."

"Can I ask you something else?"

"You can ask me anything."

"Why would you hire your ex-girlfriend?"

"I didn't hire her. My father did. He had no idea we dated. I never told him about her." No girl in the past had ever been worthy enough for me to talk about or take home to meet my family. I place my iPhone in my pocket and take both of her hands in mine. "Believe me, Lilah and I are over. I have no feelings for her. We only interact at work and it's only work related stuff we discuss."

"I don't think she's over you."

"I don't give a fuck. She means nothing to me."

"Does she know about us?"

"We agreed to be discreet in the office. There's no possibility that she would know about us unless she's following us outside of the office. No one knows about us except for Brad, and he won't say a word." Cari finally met Brad last weekend when we decided to have a combined dinner so that I could get to know Rodrigo and Hunter better, and she could get to know Brad.

"I'm real sorry I didn't tell you about her. It never crossed my mind, and even if it did it's not a big deal. She has no significance in my life."

She withdraws her hands and digs into her bag pulling out her house keys. "Of course to you it's not a big deal. Your ex and I are both working for you. How awkward is that? Can't you see how messed up this is?"

"Let's go in and finish discussing this in private please."

She unlocks the door and I follow her in. There is nothing but silence as we take the elevator up. I didn't think Lilah would be an issue between us.

"If I had told you about Lilah, could you honestly tell me you wouldn't have felt uncomfortable anyway?" I ask her.

"It would have been uncomfortable regardless. You could have at least been upfront with me about your relationship with her. I shouldn't have had to find out through other people."

She's right. "I'm sorry."

The elevator dinged to signal we have arrived on the fifth floor. She unlocks the door, and places her keys and bag on the kitchen counter. I lock the door behind me.

"Cari, look at me." She refuses to turn around. I grab her shoulders and turn her around to face me. "Please forgive me. What happened with Lilah is in the past. I don't want the past to come between us." I've never pleaded with a girl before for forgiveness. What the fuck is she doing to me? She nods her head and I'm forgiven. I stroke her jawline with my knuckles. "Let me take you out to dinner tonight."

"I'm not in the mood to go out with my headache. I just want to shower and go to bed."

"I'm not letting you go to bed without dinner. You have to eat."

She rolls her eyes at me. "Alright. Can you order the kung pao chicken for me from the Chinese take-out while I go shower?"

"Of course. Will Rodrigo be joining us for dinner?"

"No. He's out late tonight. The menus are in the top drawer next to the refrigerator," she says and heads to the bathroom.

~ * ~

CARI

I stare at myself in the mirror while the water warms up. Everett had left me so damaged. I never thought I would be able to move on yet I have. For the first time in my life I have a very intelligent, very wealthy, and very attractive man that wants to be with me for me. He has not forced me into anything, and has been nothing but wonderful to me. I know he wasn't deliberately trying to hurt me by not mentioning his past relationship with Lilah. In the short time we've been together, he's never given me any reason not to trust him. I'm not being fair to Deven either by keeping my past with Everett from him. *The past is the past.* Why resurrect it and spoil what is good between us now? She's his past. I need to put this to rest.

I walk into the dining area after the soothing shower, and see dinner is here.

"Thanks for ordering and setting up."

"You don't have to thank me." He pulls out the chair for me. I sit down and he places a kiss on the top of my head. I look up at him and see adoration in his eyes. He cares about me and that's good enough for me.

Deven offers to help me clean up after dinner, but I refuse his help. He takes out his phone and goes into the living room. After cleaning up, I go to join him on the couch only to find him sound asleep. Gosh, he's beautiful even when he's asleep. I can't bear to wake him up so I leave him sleeping on the couch. I grab an extra blanket from my room and cover him with it. I bend down to give him a kiss on his cheek, but he doesn't stir.

"Good night, Deven."

I take one more look at the beautiful man sleeping on my couch before heading back to my room. I send a quick text to Rodrigo letting him know Deven is asleep on the couch and to not disturb him when he returns. Rodrigo replies with a smiley faces and tells me he may crash at Hunter's. I put my phone down, and close my eyes and slowly drift into a deep slumber.

CHAPTER TWENTY-TWO

DEVEN

I open one eye and see sunlight filtering in through the blinds. I sit up and see a blanket over me. It takes a second to register that I'm still at Cari's. I look down at my watch. It's only six in the morning. I scrub my hands down my face, push the blanket off, and go to Cari's room. Her bedroom door is ajar. I sit on the edge of her bed and lean over to drop a kiss on her cheek. She stirs and opens her brilliant green eyes.

"Hmm…good morning." She sits up and pulls the sheet over her chest.

"Good morning, baby doll. I must have been exhausted last night."

"It was a long day yesterday. I'm glad you spent the night here even though…" She doesn't finish her sentence and her cheeks turn pink.

"Even though what?" She shakes her head. "Come on angel, tell me."

"I wish you had spent the night next to me instead."

Me too. My lips curl into a smile. "Is that so?"

"Hmm-mmm."

No longer able to resist, I bring my lips to hers. The sheet drops between us as she slides her arms around my neck and lies back down pulling me with her. She weaves her fingers into my hair without breaking our kiss. We continue to kiss until our breaths become uneven. Her taut nipples are visible through the paper thin top of hers, and it's taking a lot of self-control to not hurry to home plate right now. She slides her hands under my shirt and begins to slowly trace my abs with her fingers setting my body ablaze. *I'm in trouble.* My dick is hard as a rock.

I swiftly remove my shirt. I lean over her again, and reach under her top to cup her breast. I love how perfectly her breast molds to my hand. My fingers tease her hardened nipples while my nose and mouth skim down her neck. She lets out a soft whimper, and it sounds so sweet. I want her so badly, but I know she's not ready yet. God have mercy on me. I break away from her lips.

"Come back with me to my place?"

She lets out a shaky breath. "I thought we're going to the movies."

"We are, but I'd like to go home, shower, and change into some clean clothes first."

She places her hand on my chest. "Okay."

"Will you spend the night with me? I promise to bring you back tomorrow."

She bites her lip as she thinks it over. *Please say yes.* "I'd like that."

"Great. I'll have Mauricio come and get us at ten."

"I'll go make us some breakfast."

"Sounds good." I raise myself off of her and grab my shirt.

"What's that?" I follow her gaze. "You have a tattoo?"

"Yeah." I turn so she can get a better look at it. It's the only tattoo I have…a scroll with the Latin phrase, 'Semper Ad Meliora' inside it.

"'Always towards better things'."

She never ceases to amaze me. "Quite right Miss Snow." And being with her is towards better things.

She runs a finger along my tattoo making me tremble. Oh, fuck me.

"I like it. I have a tattoo as well."

I lift my eyebrows in surprise. "Do you?"

She bites her lower lip and nods. "It's a small one. Rodrigo convinced me to get a tattoo with him a couple of years ago."

"Can I see it?"

"It's really nothing."

"Don't get coy on me now."

She pushes down the sheet and raises the hem of her shorts to expose a pretty butterfly tattoo on her inner left thigh. *Damn that is sexy.*

"I think it's sexy where you have it." I trace the butterfly with my finger and stare into her eyes. She pushes my hair behind my ears.

"What are you thinking about?" she asks me.

"You."

"Good thoughts?"

"There is nothing but goodness when it comes to you." Her cheeks turn a lovely shade of pink. It's fucking adorable when she blushes. I give her a chaste kiss. "Okay beautiful. I'm starving."

"Kale and cheese omelet okay?"

"Never had one before."

"It's kind of like a spinach and cheese omelet."

"If you're making it I'm sure it's going to be delicious."

She rises out of bed, and I'm right behind her admiring her nice tight bumper as she walks to the kitchen. I lean against the countertop and watch as she takes out the ingredients needed to make the omelet. Having a girlfriend cook for me is a novelty…a sweet one at it. She's works fast, and the omelet is ready in a matter of minutes. She places the omelet on a plate, and pulls out a fork from one of the drawers. I put a piece of it in my mouth.

"Mmmm. This is delicious." My girl can cook.

"Thank you."

"Where is your omelet?"

"I'm not a fan of breakfast remember?"

"I do, but you have to have some kind of nourishment in the morning."

"Coffee is – "

"Not nourishment." I push some of the omelet onto my fork, and bring it to her mouth. She reluctantly opens it and chews.

"I made the omelet for you."

"And I'm sharing it with you. Besides I enjoy feeding you."

After breakfast, she packs an overnight bag and leaves a note for Rodrigo. On the drive to my penthouse she rests her head on my shoulder. I hear her softly breathe as I stare out the window. My angel is asleep. If tonight goes as well as I hope it does, I want her to start staying at the penthouse when I am not away on business.

~ * ~

CARI

A bolt of lightning rips through the sky lighting it up briefly. I wait in the living room for Deven while he cleans up after dinner. I look at the pictures he has on the shelves of his wall unit. There are a couple of pictures of him with a guy and a girl at the beach. The other picture is of him with his arm around a young Asian girl. I wonder who she is. I move over and admire his vast collection of mystery and thriller books.

"Find anything interesting?"

I jump at the sound of his voice. With my hand over my heart I turn back to see him leaning against the wall with his arms crossed.

"I was just admiring your collection here."

"There's more of a selection in my bedroom if you want to take a look."

"I'll look at it later."

He slowly makes his way to me. "Want to watch some TV?"

"Sure."

I want to ask him who the people are in the pictures, but change my mind. I don't want to dredge up anything from his past again so I drop it.

CHAPTER TWENTY-THREE

DEVEN

I lean back on the couch, and put my feet up on the coffee table. I pull Cari to me, and she curls up against me. Hmm…how nice this is. I can really get used to this. I channel surf until I come across an action movie we both have not seen. I kiss the top of her head and stroke her hair as we watch the movie.

My feelings for her have grown immensely since my return from Hong Kong. I don't ever want to let this perfect angel go. When the movie is over, I tip her chin up so I can look into her glimmering green eyes. I bring her wrist to my lips and leave a feathery kiss on it. "You're so beautiful, and kindhearted, and intelligent. I'm so damn lucky."

She shakes her head. "I think you're mistaken. I'm the lucky one here. You can have any woman you want, but you chose me."

"You captivated me from the first time I saw you." Her hands reach behind my neck to caress it while her tongue fondles mine. She fuels the fire burning inside me. I push her down on her back and crawl over her. I work quickly to unbutton her blouse, and unhook her bra. Fuck me. She has the most beautiful breasts I've ever seen. Starting at her neck, I work my way down to her breasts alternating between kissing and licking her soft skin. My mouth wraps around one of her stiff nipples teasing and sucking it as she lets out sweet moans. I do the same to the other nipple before making my way further down her body leaving light airy kisses on her until I reach the top of her shorts. I sit up and reach down to unbutton her shorts when she suddenly pushes me off of her.

"I can't Deven," she says.

She's not ready yet idiot. I help pull her up. "I'm sorry Cari. When I'm with you, I can't seem to control myself."

Shaking her head, she covers her eyes. "It's not you. It's me. There's something I should have told you."

She's nervous. I push her hair behind her shoulder and run a finger along her jaw. "What is it?"

"I'm not really into premarital sex." My eyes grow wide. *Oh shit. She's a virgin.*

Cari bites her lip and looks away embarrassed. I wrap her in my arms. "It's fine." Her admission does not change my feelings for her. It makes me cherish her even more. She's saving herself for that special someone.

"I can't give you what you want."

"Stop right there. I have what I want, and that's you."

"But you have needs."

Which man doesn't? But I will not push her. For Cari, I will wait as long as I have to…she is worth it. "I can control my needs." I'm just about to kiss her when she lets out a yawn. "I think someone is tired."

"Yes."

"Come."

I take her hand and lead her down the hall to my bedroom. "I'm going to finish up on some work. I usually work into the early morning. I'll sleep in the guest room so I don't disturb you." It's not the sleeping arrangement I prefer, but after what just happened I think it's best if we sleep apart tonight. "Your overnight bag is in the closet, and the bathroom should have everything you need." Earlier, I took a picture of the products she has in her bathroom and had Mauricio purchase the same products prior to returning home.

"You're so thoughtful." She draws me into a long and sweet kiss.

The first step to making my girlfriend feel at home is a success.

~ * ~

CARI

My body was singing with desire. I thought I was ready. I thought I could handle it, but as soon as he started to unbutton my shorts the fear and the memories came back. There was a part of me that knew Deven would do nothing to hurt me yet I still couldn't go through with it. I cannot allow those awful memories to take over me. It's held me hostage long enough. I have to move past it.

I walk into his closet to take some of my stuff out of my overnight bag. Holy cow! His custom built closet is twice the size of my bedroom. There's so much space. In the middle of the floor sits a closet island and leather bench where my overnight bag is. All the hanging space is filled with his suits. Goodness, he has a lot of suits. Does he ever wear the same suit twice?

I am astonished to see he has all of the same products I use in his bathroom. When did he have time to get all of this? Could he have been planning this for a while? I press the button to fog up the bathroom windows, and then turn on the water and step into the enormous shower.

I climb into his bed after the shower, but I can't fall asleep. I get out of bed and go next door to the connecting reading room. I look through his bookshelves, and come across the *Harry Potter* series. He likes Harry Potter? I did not peg him to be a Harry Potter fan. Grabbing the first book in the series I curl up in the chair, and start to read until my eyes shut.

~ * ~

DEVEN

I turn off the lights in my home office. I step into the hallway and see the door to my bedroom is open. I go in to check on Cari. The bed is empty, but the lights in the reading room are on. I walk in to find her asleep on the chair with a *Harry Potter* book opened on her lap. I close the book and place it on the table. I lift her into my arms, and carry her to my bed. She stirs and opens her eyes slightly. I lay her down, and sit beside her.

I brush some of her silky strands of hair away from her face. "You fell asleep reading."

"Oh." She rests her hand on her forehead. "I was having difficulty falling asleep so I thought I would read instead."

"I saw the door opened and came in to check on you. I didn't mean to wake you. Go back to sleep." I kiss her forehead and get off the bed.

She grabs my hand. "Deven?"

"Yes, baby doll?"

"I don't want you to sleep in a different room. I want you here with me."

"You're sure?"

She nods. There's no way I am refusing her request. I strip out of my shirt and pants, and get into bed with her. I shut off the lights, and close my eyes.

"Will you hold me Deven?"

I roll onto my side and pull her into my arms. I love having her in my bed, in my arms, and in my life. I plant a kiss on her shoulder, and succumb to the most peaceful sleep I have had in a long time.

CHAPTER TWENTY-FOUR

CARI

Deven and I have settled into a familiar pattern. I spend the weekends and one weeknight at his penthouse, and three times during the work week we meet for dinner after work.

Tonight, Deven wanted to whip up a delicious dinner for us after work instead of going out. After a scrumptious meal of veal scaloppini, we snuggle on the couch and watch *The Bachelor*. Deven claims to hate the show, but I think he secretly loves it. Sometimes I still find it surreal that I am dating one of the hottest and most eligible bachelors. We've been dating for nearly two months and I have yet to meet his family.

"You don't say much about your family."

He rubs his hand up and down my back. "Not much to say. You already know I have a younger sister. Dad adopted her from China when she was a few months old." His sister must be the Asian girl that I saw in the picture on his shelf. "I have a stepmother, and you're aware of my father's condition."

"What about your birth mom?"

His jaw tightens. "I only speak to her when she needs something. She remarried and lives in Paris with her fourth husband. My half-siblings and I share the same mother."

"Your half-siblings that live on the west coast?"

"Yes. They moved out there as they both wanted to go to college in California."

"You must see them a lot when you're there."

"More recently now than before."

"Where did they study?"

"My half-brother is finishing his master's program at UCLA, and my half-sister dropped out of college to pursue an acting career."

"What is your half-brother studying?"

"Education. He wants to be a high school teacher. I offered him a very lucrative package to work in my company, but he refused it. He rather teach." Deven seems perturbed at his brother's decision.

"And your half-sister?"

He shrugs. "She only has small roles right now."

"She doesn't want to work for the company?"

He shakes his head. "She's not the right fit." He does not elaborate why she is not the right fit.

"Well, I hope I can meet them some day."

"The next time they come to New York I will see that you do, but first I want you to meet my mother and sister."

Can this man read my mind? "You do?"

"Yes, I do. They've been asking when they can meet you, but I want to be certain you're ready."

"I am."

"How about next Sunday?"

"Next Sunday is perfect."

"Good. They're going to love you."

That's what I'm hoping.

~ * ~

Our first stop on Sunday is to visit Deven's father. It is hard to miss the warm ambiance and friendly staff at the care center. Deven gives me a tour of the well-maintained premises before we visit his father. His father's room is quite large. There's a small sitting area with a couch and a chair on the other side of the room. A few pictures of his family and a couple of books are on the table next to his bed.

"Good morning, Dad." He leans down to give his father a kiss on the cheek. His father is hooked up to an IV, and looks frail. With some difficulty his father pats Deven's hand.

"Dad, I brought along someone very special." I go to stand beside Deven. "This is my girlfriend that I have been telling you about. Her name is Cari."

"It's very nice to meet you Mr. Blake." I extend my hand, but instead of shaking it he stares at it. Deven advised earlier not to take offense to anything he may say or do that is rude or insulting. Remembering that, I let my hand drop.

Deven motions for me to take a seat. It's endearing to watch Deven with his father. He updates his father on the latest in the real estate world of BG. At times, his father attempts to respond to Deven, but the words come out slurred. Somehow Deven comprehends everything his father says. We stay for a while. Deven makes sure his father takes his prescribed medicine, and once his father dozes off we leave. Next stop is Greenwich.

We approach a pair of tall black arched iron gates. Deven opens his window to punch in the code. The entrance gates part to a sweeping tree line road, and acres of landscaped grounds. The long road ultimately leads into a cobblestone courtyard with a tiered water fountain in the center, and behind it stood a magnificent French inspired mansion.

"Welcome to the Blake Estate," Deven says as we enter the house. He places the cake I bought on a table.

Manners abandoned, my mouth hangs open as I take in the grandeur of the foyer. A round carved marble table with gold accents reminiscent of eighteenth century France rests in the center, and high above it hangs an oversized ornate glass chandelier. But it's the sweeping double staircase and wrought iron banister that commands the attention of this vestibule.

"Deven!"

I turn around to see a pretty young Asian girl run into his arms.

"Hey, May." He hugs her and places a kiss on the top of her head.

"Hey big brother." She angles her head to the side. "Is that her?"

"Yes. This is my girlfriend, Cari. Cari, allow me to introduce you to my baby sister Mayleen."

She playfully punches his arm. "I'm *not* a baby. Hi, Cari." She hugs me.

I'm pleasantly surprised by her friendliness. "I've been waiting like forever to meet you."

She's sweet, and I like her already. "It's nice to finally meet you."

"She's very pretty," Mayleen whispers to Deven making him smile.

"I know." Hearing his reply makes my cheeks blush. "Where's mom?"

"She's in the kitchen."

"I want to introduce you to my Mom first before I give you the tour of the house." He takes the cake in one hand, and grabs my hand with his free hand. He leads me through a room and down the hallway into the spacious gourmet kitchen.

"Hi, Mom. Look who I brought home." Deven puts the cake in the commercial grade refrigerator.

A beautiful woman with honey blonde hair, and warm brown eyes comes up to me. "You must be Cari."

"Yes, I am."

"Cari, this is my mom, Leigh."

"It's a pleasure to meet you Mrs. Blake." I offer a handshake, but she embraces me instead.

"It's lovely to meet you Cari, and please, call me Leigh."

"Mom, Cari brought a cake. I put it in the fridge."

"Why that's so nice of you Cari. Thank you."

"I'm going to show her the house while you finish up here."

"Sure. See you two shortly."

Deven puts an arm around me and starts off in the basement. The ostentatious mansion is nothing short of splendid from the custom woodcarvings and moldings to the opulent furnishings. *This is as close as I will ever get to the Palace of Versailles.* We make it to the second floor where all eight bedrooms are located. We walk past a set of doors as we go across the hall.

"Is that an elevator?" I ask.

"It is. It goes to the basement." No expense had been spared on this house. He stops in front of a door at the end of the hall. "This is my room." He opens the door letting me go in first. A trophy case displaying various awards occupies one side of the wall, autographed pictures of athletes and a couple of celebrities are hung on another.

"The room hasn't changed much since I left for college." He shrugs. "Mom and Dad didn't want to change anything."

There are a few frames on his desk, and I walk over to get a closer look. One picture is of the family on a beach, and the other is of Deven graduating college looking just as gorgeous then as he does now.

"That picture was taken in Hawaii." He points to the family photo. "It was our last family vacation together."

"How long ago was that?"

"Three years ago." Mr. Blake looked so much younger and healthier then. Deven sits down on his bed and requests I sit next to him. "There's something I want to ask you."

"What is it?"

"How would you like to go away with me next weekend?"

"Where to?"

"Newport. We have a house there, and it would be just us."

A weekend alone in Newport sounds romantic. "I'd love to go."

"Good. We can leave right after work."

"I'll be ready." I wrap my arms around his neck. He leans into me and presses his lips to mine. Within a few seconds he has me on my back and raises himself above me. He trails kisses down my neck, and I feel his arousal as he slowly lies on top of me.

"If we don't stop this now I don't think I'll be able to stop at all." He gets up and helps me off the bed. I run my hands through my hair and smooth it back into place. Lacing his fingers with mine we leave his bedroom and he brings me to the back of the house.

The stone veranda extends the entire length of the house. A couple of loveseats and chairs surround a fire pit in the center of the veranda, and on one end of the veranda is an outdoor kitchen complete with a built-in grill. The view of the sprawling lawns leaves me breathless. The pool and pool house are several feet away separated by a stone wall. His cell phone rings as we approach the house from our tour of the pool. He pulls it out of his pocket to see who is calling.

"I have to take this call. Be right back."

"I'll be here." I smile at him.

He smiles back before going into the house to answer the call. "This better be important."

I take a seat on the loveseat and enjoy the serene surroundings.

"Hi again." I turn and see Mayleen take a seat opposite of me.

"My brother left you here by yourself?"

"He had to take a call."

Mayleen rolls her eyes. "Work as usual. Did he show you around?"

"Yes, he did. It's really beautiful here."

She shrugs. "It's okay. Some of my friends live in houses larger than this. You know, you're the first girl my brother has ever talked about, and the first one he has ever brought home to meet us."

Well, that's news. "Really?"

"Uh-huh. You're special. He's so into you."

"He's a great guy."

She nods and laughs. "He is. My friends are so jealous of you."

"Of me? Why?"

"You snatched up my brother. They're all crushing on him."

Deven returns at that moment and plops down beside me.

"I'm sorry about that."

"Deven, you are so rude! You ignored your girlfriend to take that call?"

He puts an arm around me and kisses my temple. "I'm not ignoring her now. Forgive me Cari?"

Before I can answer him, Leigh announces dinner is ready. Mayleen is the first to go in. Deven and I follow right behind. The food looks and smells delicious making my mouth water. His mother made chateaubriand with several accompanying sides. I cut a piece of my chateaubriand and throw it in my mouth. *Hmm.*

"How do you like working at BG?" his mother asks me.

"It's wonderful. I'm learning a lot, and everyone is very nice."

"You must see each other a lot," May says.

"On the contrary baby sis. My day is usually booked. You can always come and work for me. I can give you half of my workload and then I can spend more time with my lovely girl."

I blush at his comment.

"You should spend more time with Cari regardless, but I don't want to work at BG."

Watching the exchange between the two siblings is entertaining.

"Mayleen, I understand you're going into your senior year."

"Yes, finally. I've waited so long to become a senior."

"It will be an exciting year for you. Have you decided which college you are applying to?"

Deven snorts and we all look at him.

"Sorry."

Mayleen narrows her eyes at him. "He's just annoyed because I am not going to U Penn."

"Which school do you want to go to?"

"Princeton."

"She wants to become a writer instead of going into the family business," Deven explains.

"Are you interested in writing books or articles?"

"I don't know yet. I just like writing."

"Maybe you can be my PR rep. We need someone to write press releases."

She makes a face.

"That's a rather good idea. I like it," Leigh says making Mayleen sigh loudly. Apparently Mayleen wants no part of the empire Mr. Blake created.

I was nervous about meeting his mother and sister. I did not know what to expect, but it turns out they're really down-to-earth. And like Deven, they made me feel comfortable immediately. After dessert, Deven and I bid farewell. They made Deven promise not to be selfish and to bring me by again soon.

"They loved you."

"They are wonderful. Thank you for arranging this."

He reaches for my hand.

"Silly girl. Why are you thanking me? I'm glad they finally got to meet you. You're the first girl that I have ever brought home to meet my family."

"That's what your sister said."

"In fact, you're the first girl that I have ever brought back to the penthouse."

What? I can't believe he's never brought anyone up to his penthouse before. That would mean he's never shared his bed with anyone else either. Wow. *I must mean a lot to him.* I stare out my window into the dark sky.

"So if your grandparents were still alive, would they have approved of me?"

I turn and look at him. "Oh, definitely. You would have charmed the pants off of Grams."

He laughs. "Nice to know." He squeezes my hand. "I wish I could have met them, but I have a feeling they're watching me from above anyhow."

And I'm sure they approve and are smiling down on both of us.

CHAPTER TWENTY-FIVE

September

CARI

At five on the dot I leave the office to head home and pack for my weekend trip with Deven. He has some work to finish up in the office and will come to get me at seven. I toss the small suitcase onto my bed and pack a few outfits. Rodrigo comes into my room and watches as I pack.

"I think this is it."

Rodrigo arches an eyebrow. "I think that's all you need for a weekend trip."

"No. I mean *this is it.*"

"What are you talking about?"

"I'm going to sleep with Deven this weekend."

"Sweetie, you have been *sleeping* with him every weekend."

"I mean I'm going to let him make love to me."

Rodrigo's eyes widen. "That's a huge step. Are you ready?"

"I am. I can do this. I'm not going to let that fear control me. And a man has his needs after all."

"Amen to that."

"Deven's been incredibly patient with me. He hasn't forced me to do anything against my will, and he's willing to wait as long as he has to."

"Honey, if he finds out what that douchebag did to you he may never touch you again."

I cross my arms. I don't want to think about those horrible memories.

"He never has to know. It's taken me a while to overcome what happened. I don't want it to ruin what's good between Deven and I."

"I know sweetie. You have come a long way. This is long overdue."

"I feel like I can really move on now, and it's all because of Deven. I'm falling in love with him."

Rodrigo puts hand over his heart. "Oh, that's so sweet. He's good for you, and he's good to you."

"He is."

"I have something for you. I'll be right back."

While he goes to get whatever it is he has for me, I go into the bathroom to grab my toothbrush and toothpaste. When I return to my room, Rodrigo is sitting on my bed. My eyes spot the condoms beside my suitcase.

He picks up a packet. "You need to have plenty of these on hand if you plan on having sex with him."

My cheeks must be deep scarlet by now. "Rodrigo, I'm sure he has some."

"How do you know? Did you tell him you plan on having sex with him?"

"No, but he's a man. And men always carry condoms in their wallet, don't they?"

He wags his finger at me. "Not all men my dear. And you don't know if he is clean. Best be safe."

He's right. I don't know how many girls he has slept with in the past. "Fine. I'll pack them." I stuff the condoms in the bottom of my make-up bag. *How much sex does he think we're going to have?*

"It's been a while since you've had any kind of penetration there so you might be sore afterwards."

"Ewww!" I say as I cover my ears.

Rodrigo rolls his eyes. "Stop being childish about this. We're adults now. Are you still on birth control?"

"Yes, I am." God, Rodrigo can be so overprotective.

"Good. Did you have your vajayjay waxed?"

"Oh my God Rodrigo! That is none of your business!" I refuse to discuss such intimate details with him.

"Heterosexual men like it bald there."

I put my hand up. "That is the end of this conversation."

By the time I am done packing and showering, it is almost seven. Prompt as usual, Deven comes up to the apartment to get me, and carries my suitcase down. He jokes that I shouldn't have packed much as we would probably stay in bed a lot. Does he know what I have planned?

We hit some patches of traffic on the way to Newport, and darkness takes over by the time we arrive. Just like his parents' house, Deven stops in front of a gate and punches in a code to open them. Old-fashioned kerosene lamps light up the driveway as he drives towards the house and pulls into one of the four garages.

"Dad tore the previous house down and built this. I'll show you the grounds tomorrow and the fantastic view of the ocean." He grabs our bags from the back of his Jaguar and takes me into the house. He turns the lights on, and sets our bags down in the hallway.

Deven shows me the first floor of the house, and goes to get our bags. The house is not quite as large as their house in Greenwich, but it is just as beautiful and impressive.

"Our room." He flicks the light switch on, and places our bags in front of the luggage racks.

The room is enormous with a poster bed, and a fireplace. There's also a set of French doors which open to a balcony.

"I like the balcony."

"Want to step outside?"

I nod. Deven flips on the light switch for the balcony and we step out. The balcony is spacious and furnished with two chaise lounge chairs and a table. I wonder what it would be like to make love under the stars.

"You're going to love the view when you see it during the day. Why don't you unpack while I make dinner?" Deven asks breaking me away from the thought.

I stand on my toes, wrap my arms around his neck, and kiss him. "You are incredible. You work all day, drive here, and now you're going to cook? We could go out."

He pulls me tighter to him. "I love doing things for you and cooking is not a big deal. Come down when you're done."

"I will."

He lifts my bag and puts it on the luggage rack for me, and then leaves to make dinner. I search for an empty dresser drawer to put away my clothes. I take out the mauve chemise I purchased for this weekend, and hold the sheer fabric against me. My gaze shifts to the king size poster bed where we will be making love. I swallow and close my eyes. *I can do this.*

The smell of dinner has me unpacking quickly. I follow the delicious scent to the kitchen, and watch Deven stir the pot.

"It smells delicious."

"Why thank you. Dinner's almost ready."

He has two place settings and two glasses of red wine on the island. I pull out a stool and sit down. Deven plates the food and brings our dinner to the island sitting in the chair next to me. He made ravioli tossed with asparagus and pine nuts. I'm famished and dig into my food immediately.

He chuckles. "Hungry?"

I swallow my ravioli. "I didn't realize how famished I was until I got a whiff of dinner which incidentally is delicious as always."

"Thank you."

After dinner we clean up the kitchen, and then head up to our room. Deven goes to shower. While Deven is in the shower, I change into my chemise. It is the sexiest thing I have ever bought for myself. Feeling nervous I step outside. I walk out onto the balcony and lean on the railing. I inhale the ocean air. The stars are shining brightly on this clear and tranquil night, and the night air is crisp and a bit nippy making goose bumps appear on my arms. The only noise out there is the sound of the waves crashing gently against the seawall.

"What are you doing out here?" Deven comes up behind me sliding his arms around my waist. I lean back against him and he nibbles my ear.

"Let's go back inside. It's a bit cool out here."

He releases me and pulls me back into the room closing the balcony door behind us. The lights in the room have been dimmed. He gently places his fingers under my chin and lifts my face up. Those smoldering eyes of his make my skin scorching hot. I press my palms flat against his muscular, sculpted bare chest. Slowly I start to trace my fingers over his washboard abs. I watch as his eyelids flutter from my touch, his arousal becoming evident, and his breathing starting to become shallow. I'm filled with throbbing desire. I'm so ready for this…for him.

CHAPTER TWENTY-SIX

DEVEN

She is a dream come true. Cari practically naked has me wanting to fuck her right now. Her lovely tits are spilling over, and her panties hide nothing. The combination of her and the lack of sex I haven't had in months have made me extremely hungry.

I'm about to tell her how much I want her, but she places her finger over my lips to silence me. She lies back on the bed, and I climb on hovering over her. My dick is so hard the seams in my pants are about to burst.

"Deven," she says hooking her desperate eyes onto mine as she runs her fingers along the stubble on my face. "I want you to make love to me."

I look at her. She's ready and willing to give her virginity to me?

"Are you sure Cari? I don't want you to feel pressured into doing something you're not ready for."

She places her hands on my cheeks. "Yes, I'm sure. And I'm ready. Just don't hurt me."

Hurt her? Never. "You're so precious to me Cari. I would never hurt you. Trust me love."

"I trust you."

She trusts me to take what's precious from her, and make her completely mine. God, how I cherish this beautiful girl. I slide her nightie off setting her plump breasts free. My hands cup her voluptuous globes before gliding down her body to remove her panties. My God. She is a sight to behold as she lies before me magnificently nude. She's stunning, and perfect with an amazing body and curves in all the right places.

"You take my breath away Cari."

I raise myself off of her to remove my pants. I catch her eyes grow wide at the sight of me in the nude. I smile inwardly, and lay on top of her. I stroke her inner thigh, and she tenses up. My eyes dart back to hers. "Are you okay?"

"Yeah," she whispers. "Don't stop. Please don't stop."

"I'm just getting started baby doll. Let me love you."

"That's what I want."

My fingers journey back down her inner thigh stroking it lightly along the way. Her head tilts back as she draws in deep breaths. I kiss her breasts and nuzzle them. Moving south, I place my face between her legs, and lick her folds. Damn, she tastes good. I pleasure her some more as I tease, taste, and suck on her clit. I watch her come undone as my mouth is sucking on her sweetness.

"Deven," she calls my name between ragged breaths.

I move back over her and brush her hair back. She looks at me through hooded eyes while I slide a finger into her slick opening. I slide another finger in her and she arches her back and moans. Such a sweet sound. She's so fucking wet. I pull my fingers out and position myself to enter her. I am inches from making both of our dreams come true when I realize I don't have a condom. Shit! I shake my head in disbelief.

"What's wrong?"

"I don't have protection."

"I'm on birth control, and I brought some condoms in case," she says shyly.

My eyes widen in surprise. My angel came prepared. The inward smile is back. I should put a condom on, but I know we're both clean. She's a virgin, and I haven't gotten laid in months. When I was sexually active I always wore a condom and made sure I got tested on a regular basis for any STD's just to be on the safe side. But with Cari, the rules have changed. Do I dare to go bareback?

"I want to do something I've never done before."

"What's that?"

"I have a clean bill of health, and I'm sure you do too."

"I do."

"Good. Since you're on birth control I want to forgo the condom, but only if you're okay with it."

Her eyes are full of trust as her hands cover my ass. "I trust you Deven."

I brush my stiff cock against her pretty pussy. She tightens her legs around my waist and strokes my back. I penetrate only the tip of my dick into her and make sure she is not uncomfortable or hurt. I want her first time to be special, and unforgettable, not painful.

"Cari, are you okay?"

"Yeah," she whispers back.

That's all she needs to say before I completely push into her slick tight pussy. She lets out a cry of pleasure. The sensation of being inside of her without any protection is pure heaven. Our mouths crash together needing, wanting, and taking. She rocks with me, and it's absolute fucking bliss. I don't want this to end. Our naked bodies move together in perfect sync as we continue to touch and taste each other. I lick her, and she licks back. I suck on her skin, and she sucks back on mine. I rest my forehead on hers and intertwine our fingers. Her eyes fixate on mine and I can see all of her emotions in her gorgeous eyes. Love, lust, passion, and desire. I thrust deeper losing myself completely in her as she cries out my name repeatedly. *This is orgasm heaven.* She shudders, and it's only a little longer before I explode inside her like lava erupting from a volcano. We cling to each other as we catch our breaths. *I'm clinging to a girl. I've never clung to a girl after sex.*

It's never felt like this before. *Never.* There are no words to describe how perfect that was between us. *None.* I am hers, and she is mine. I lay on top of her for a moment longer before shifting myself onto the bed pulling her to me. She rests her head on my shoulder, and splays her hand on my chest.

"How are you feeling? Any discomfort?"

"No. I'm fine." She peers up at me. "I'd like to do it again."

And I want to honor her request, but I know it's too soon. I kiss the top of her head. "So would I, but you may be a bit sore."

"I am a little sore. Maybe later then?"

"I'll be ready and waiting."

She wraps her arm around me and snuggles up to me. Sex before Cari was meaningless. And cuddling? Non-existent. Everything I do with Cari means so much more. She's it for me. I live for her, and can't imagine my life without her. She had me from the moment I first laid eyes on her, and I want her to know how I feel. I cannot help this euphoric feeling. No better than the present moment to tell her. I run a finger up and down her arm, but she does not stir. I look down and she's asleep.

"I love you Carilyn Jade," I whisper softly and close my eyes.

CHAPTER TWENTY-SEVEN

CARI

I wake up to find the bed empty. Sitting up and stretching I think back to last night. I didn't know sex could be so good. Deven made me feel loved, cherished, beautiful, and sexy. He was huge yet he was gentle and careful with me even when the moment became frenzied. A smile stretches across my face as I walk over to the dresser and pull out one of his t-shirts. I throw it on, and brush my teeth before going downstairs.

"Ah, perfect timing." He slides the scrambled eggs onto the plates and sets them on the table. Just as I'm about to sit down, he grabs me and kisses me. This man is intoxicating.

"Let's eat." We sit down and start to eat. "How are you feeling?"

"Very good."

"No discomfort then?"

I shake my head. "No discomfort. Last night was incredible. I hope it was the same for you."

"Of course it was angel. Why wouldn't it have been?" He looks quizzically at me.

I shrug. "You've slept with other women who are more experienced than I am. I don't know if I can ever measure up to them. I –"

"That's enough. Making love to you last night was un-fucking-believable. It was the best night I ever had. I don't care about any of those other women. They mean nothing to me, but you Cari, you mean everything to me." He brings my hand to his lips and kisses the top of it. "Don't compare yourself to them. I love you, and I care about you. You're the one I want to be with."

Why do I always doubt myself, or compare myself to those other women? "I'm sorry Deven."

"Stop apologizing. Never think so low of yourself, okay? You're gorgeous, intelligent, sweet, and caring. I love you."

My heart seizes. He just told me he loves me. I lean forward and give him two chaste kisses. "I love you too."

He raises his eyebrows and he smiles that sexy smile of his. "Yeah?"

"Yeah."

"I love hearing you say that. And just for the record, I haven't slept with a lot of women." I close my eyes and breathe a sigh of relief. "I had plans to take you into town, but seeing you in my shirt is making me reconsider." He dips his head and kisses me. My hands reach around his back pressing him closer to me.

"Deven?"

"Hmm?"

"I want a repeat performance of last night."

He instantly sweeps me off my feet and carries me back up to the bedroom placing me down gently on the bed. He pulls off his shirt, and strips out of his pajama bottoms. Just like last night I am left breathless at the sight of him naked. Every inch of him is beautiful and perfect. I take off the t-shirt I have on. His tongue swirls circles around my nipples, and then moves to take each of my breasts in his mouth. He spreads my legs wider with his knee and kisses his way down until he reaches my sensitive area. I look down through my long lashes, and see the top of his head as his tongue works its magic.

"Now. Please Deven," I beseech him.

He crawls back up to me. His lustful blue eyes hold my eyes captive as he hovers over me. Pinning my arms above my head he effortlessly slides inside, filling me. I like that there are no barriers between us. It makes our connection more intense.

"So fucking beautiful." He nuzzles my neck. "So good together." He slams into me sending waves of pleasure through me. *He feels so good inside of me.* His breathing becomes labored and it won't be much longer before this moment ends. We climax simultaneously leaving us both shuddering and holding onto each other.

Deven slowly rolls off of me, and we lie in bed together. His strong muscular arms wrap around me and hold me close to him. We stay like this until he asks me to join him in the shower. Is that what couples do after they have sex? He leaves the bed and heads into the bathroom to warm up the shower. I come in shortly after. I open the door to the shower and wrap my arms around his trim waist pressing my cheek against his back as the water rains down on us. He turns around and I am shocked to see his manhood is standing to attention.

"Like what you see?"

I nod. His hands firmly grip my waist as he lowers his mouth to mine. He releases his hands from my waist, and his fingers skim my body turning up the heat inside of me. *I am about to combust.* His hands cup my ass and he lifts me up, pushing me against the shower wall. My legs hitch around his waist and I hold onto him tight as he pounds into me. In and out, hard and fast.

"I. Can't. Get. Enough. Of. You," Deven says as he pushes deeper into me until we both come. He loosens his grip on me and lowers me. My legs can barely support me. As soon as he catches his breath, he squirts some soap into his hands and starts to wash me clean worshipping my body as he does. *Holy cow.* This is the best shower I ever had.

CHAPTER TWENTY-EIGHT

DEVEN

After our morning fuck in bed and in the shower, I show her the grounds of the Newport estate. She stops at the stone wall and stares out into the ocean. The breeze blows her hair away from her face and she looks absolutely breathtaking. I wish I had brought my phone with me so I could snap a picture of her.

Downtown Newport is streaming with locals, and tourists enjoying the unofficial last weekend of summer. We pass by a jewelry shop, and she stops to look at the window display. I am curious to see what caught her attention. There is a display of necklaces, rings, and bracelets. Eager to buy something for her I ask if she sees anything she likes.

"I do, but I rather not spend any money on it."

"You don't have to. I'll buy it for you. It will be my gift to you."

"I can't let you do that."

I want to buy everything her heart desires, but she refuses to let me. I have never had a woman refuse anything from me. "Why not?"

"It's your money."

"Precisely. It is my money and I can do anything I want with it. And what I want is to spend it on you."

She looks at me, tucks a strand of loose hair behind her ear and looks back at the window.

"I'm not worth spending money on."

How can she even think that? I grab her shoulders and turn her to me.

"You are so worth it." I kiss her forehead. "I'd like to think I make a somewhat decent salary, and if I choose to spend every last dime of it on you I can do so. No more discussing this. What pieces of jewelry were you eyeing?"

She points to a bracelet with some charms hanging on it. We stride into the store and I ask the sales associate to show us the bracelet. She takes the bracelet out of the case and hands it to Cari. Cari examines the bracelet carefully. There are three charms dangling…a mermaid, a sailboat, and a shell. It's a pretty bracelet, but I think a diamond bracelet will look much nicer on her wrist. The associate gives us the history of the designer of the bracelet. I tune her out and take a look at the other jewelry she is selling. I am disappointed that there is not one diamond bracelet for sale. I look back and see the associate put the bracelet away. Cari thanks her and tugs at my hand pulling me out of the store.

"Did you not like the bracelet?"

She shrugs. "I did, but it's too expensive. Let's go to the Cliff Walk now."

Traffic is heavier than usual and it takes more than a half hour to get to the Cliff Walk. We stroll hand in hand along the picturesque walk which overlooks the ocean.

"Ever been in the mansions?"

"Just the one the Astors had which is beautiful. And of course your family estate here."

I laugh. Cari has not seen anything yet. My family house is nothing compared to the mansions, especially The Breakers…the grandest mansions of them all. Maybe I can arrange a private tour of a few of the mansions tomorrow before we leave.

"Give me a second." I reach for my phone and send a quick email to the head of the Preservation Society asking for the favor. I trust she will be able to pull some strings for me. After all, my family has been quite generous in supporting them. All I want right now is to go back to the house and make love to her the rest of the day. I gaze at her lovingly before pulling her to me and kissing her. Within seconds our hands are entangled in each other's hair.

"Mommy, look! Kissing!"

I pull away from Cari, and turn to where the voice came from. I see a little girl staring wide eyed at Cari and I like we are an addicting cartoon show. Fuck. I look over to the girl's mother and she's staring at me. Great, another one who can't take her eyes off of me.

"Come on Janie," the mother finally says reaching out to grab her daughter's hand. "I'm sorry she interrupted." She smiles cordially, and walks away with her daughter.

Cari's cheeks are flaming red.

"Come. Let's go finish our walk." I put my arm around her shoulder, and we continue on.

By the time we head back to the car twilight approaches. We have dinner at one of my favorite local restaurants before going back to the house. While she brushes her teeth, I check my emails and see that my wish for a private tour at two of the mansions has been granted. Perfect. I just finish sending an email when she steps out of the bathroom wearing a tank top and shorts. I'm disappointed she's not wearing the sexy little thing she had on last night. I like her in sexy lingerie.

"Come here beautiful." I set aside my phone as she gets in bed. I hold her in my arms and kiss her neck.

"Deven?"

"Hmm?"

"Thank you for this weekend. It's been perfect."

"Stop thanking me." One day she will learn to stop thanking me. "This weekend is for us. Let's keep enjoying it." I am drunk with love for this beautiful girl. My hand pulls down one of the straps on her tank top and I place light kisses on her shoulder.

"Deven, I'm ready."

I smile. So am I. When a fine woman tells a man she is ready, a smart man waits no longer. And that's all I am saying.

CHAPTER TWENTY-NINE

Late September

CARI

Today is Alana's big day. I've never been to a wedding. Hers will be the first. Deven and I are going to go together as a couple as he no longer wants to hide our relationship at work.

I stare at the designer dress I will be wearing tonight. It's a beautiful strapless burgundy chiffon gown with a beaded lace top and a beaded waist. It cost nearly two thousand dollars. Deven had given me his credit card and insisted I purchase the dress with it. Rodrigo had accompanied me on the shopping trip, and did not hesitate to make sure I spent Deven's money.

I step into the dress, pull up the zipper, and straighten it out. Tossing my curls back, I look into the mirror, and gasp when I see my reflection. Wow! I look elegant and sophisticated. Stepping into my Louboutins, I leave the bedroom and head for the living room. Deven is talking on his cell phone while looking out the window. He turns around, and my breath catches.

He finishes up the call, and takes a few steps closer to me. "Cari." He looks at me appreciatively from head to toe making me tingle all over. "You look absolutely stunning."

"Thank you. You don't look too bad yourself Mr. Blake." I smooth out the lapels of his suit jacket.

He catches my wrists and kisses each one. "I have something for you." He takes my hand and tugs me with him down the corridor to his home office. "Close your eyes."

I do as he requests and I hear him open and close a drawer.

"Open them."

I open my eyes. *Oh my gosh!* He holds open a box containing a glittering diamond scroll bracelet.

"It's beautiful, but I can't –"

"Don't tell me you cannot accept it. You can and you will because it's my gift to you."

I shake my head. "It's too much."

"Nothing will ever be too much for you angel." He removes the sparkling bracelet from the box and puts it on my right wrist. He closes the clasp and admires the bracelet. It really is beautiful, and must have cost him a fortune.

"Beautiful. Shall we?" he asks and extends his hand. I nod and place my hand in his.

~ * ~

The wedding is being held at a swanky country club in New Jersey. Deven pulls under the porte-cochère, and puts the car in park. One of the valets come to my side and opens my door extending a hand to help me out of the Maserati Granturismo. Deven is immediately at my side and wraps a protective arm around me flashing the valet a warning look. Two doormen open the doors for us. We walk in and are directed to the room where the ceremony will take place. As I look for Rodrigo and Hunter, I see some of the people from work…Catrina, Jeremy, and Jenna. Brad unfortunately could not make it because his cousin is getting married today as well.

"Ready?" Deven whispers. He must have seen them too. "It'll be fine. If not, I'll fire all of them." Judging by his tone he is serious. He leads the way and strolls up to the BG team. They all stare at us with their mouths agape.

"Good evening everyone. It's good to see all of you here," Deven says.

We exchange greetings, and I receive compliments on how lovely I look making me blush different shades of red. No one comments on our hand holding.

"You're here!"

I turn around and see Rodrigo coming towards us with Hunter. I'm glad to see them. Rodrigo and Alana have become good friends since I first introduced them.

"Hello darling." Rodrigo embraces me and gives me a kiss on the cheek. "You look fabulous!"

"Thank you. Hi, Hunter." I hug him as well.

"You do look radiant Cari," Hunter tells me.

"Thanks."

Deven shakes their hands. Rodrigo whispers something to Deven and Deven's face lights up. Hmm…what was that about? I am delighted that my two best friends and my boyfriend get along very well. Deven introduces them to the group from BG, and we make small talk.

"Let's go in before all the seats are taken," Rodrigo says.

The BG group has already dispersed into the room. Deven and I follow Rodrigo and Hunter. I'm blown away by how beautiful the room is. It's exactly how Alana described it to be. Candles of various sizes adorn the space while the delicate scent of the flowers permeates the room. A floral covered arch is placed at the beginning of the aisle, and flower petals line the sides. In the far corner of the room sits a violinist and a guitarist.

The doors open and the groom is the first to walk down the aisle. He is smiling widely, and his smile is infectious. He takes his place and watches as his best man and his groomsmen follow behind in single file. The bridesmaids and the maid-of-honor follow suit after. The ring bearer is Alana's four-year-old nephew and he ends up running down the aisle into his father's arms while the flower girl methodically sprinkles more petals on the runner. When the music changes to the wedding march, the priest asks everyone to stand. Alana is beaming as she gracefully walks down the aisle on her father's arm. She makes a beautiful bride in her satin and tulle wedding dress.

After the ceremony, we follow the other guests to the cocktail reception. There are passed hors d'oeuvres, and stations throughout the room. I can't wait to try everything. Hunter and Rodrigo help themselves to the food being served at the stations. Deven is in line at the bar waiting to get a glass of wine for me. I wait for him by the fireplace when Jeremy approaches me.

"So Cari, you and the boss man are an item, huh?"

I blush. I am not prepared to answer any questions about Deven and I.

"Guess that means you're off the market?"

"Yes, that means she is off the market." We both turn around to see Deven standing there glaring at Jeremy. Deven hands me my glass of wine.

"That's too bad," Jeremy says.

"If you'll pardon us." Deven laces his fingers with mine and takes me to the other side of the room where Rodrigo and Hunter have secured a table. Deven pulls out the chair for me and tells me he will be right back with something for me to eat.

"I want to have a wedding like this," Rodrigo says looking at Hunter. Rodrigo is more into the glitzier and fancier things than Hunter is.

"Maybe we can take it down a notch or two. We should only have our closest family and friends," says Hunter.

Rodrigo turns to me. "If you marry Deven I can see it being a grand wedding."

"Cari, do you want a fancy wedding like this or something more intimate?" Hunter asks.

For goodness sake, I just started dating Deven and we're talking about marriage already?

"I'm curious to know too."

My face turns beet red, and Rodrigo's and Hunter's mouths both form an "o." Deven places a plate down in front of me and takes a seat.

"Oh, look Hunter. They must have brought out some more sushi. Let's go get some." Hunter and Rodrigo quickly get up and leave me alone at the table with Deven.

Deven leans closer to me. "Tell me Cari. What kind of wedding do you want?"

I shove a piece of sushi into my mouth to prolong having to answer his question. When I finish chewing, I reach for another one, but Deven grabs my fingers.

"You didn't answer my question."

"I don't have an answer."

"All girls dream about their wedding. Haven't you?"

I was never like the other girls at school, but he didn't know that. "No. Never."

His eyes widen in surprise. He takes my hand and rubs his thumb back and forth over my knuckles. "Amazing. You are the only woman I know who has never fantasized about her own wedding." He brings my hand up and tenderly kisses my knuckles.

Not too long after, we move to a different room for dinner and dancing. We are seated at the same table with Hunter and Rodrigo, and some of the team from BG.

Throughout the night Deven keeps me by his side. Deven made it clear he did not want any other guy near me, especially Jeremy. If I wasn't dancing with him, I was dancing with either Rodrigo or Hunter. After dessert, he takes me back onto the dance floor. As soon as the song is over, he puts his arm around my waist and leans into me.

"We should go. My zipper is about to bust open soon from wanting to be inside you. I'm sure no one wants to see the boss indecent."

I shake my head as we head back to the table. I grab my shawl and purse, and say goodbye to Rodrigo and Hunter first. The BG team is surprised we are leaving already, but Deven offers them no explanation. He drops the envelope for the happy couple into the well, and we line up behind the other guests who are waiting to say goodbye to the newlyweds.

"You're leaving already?" Alana asks.

"I'm sorry Alana, but I do have to get back home and review some proposals."

"Always working."

"And always will. Congratulations to the both of you again. Everything was lovely and you look beautiful Alana," Deven says giving her a kiss on the cheek, and then shaking her husband's hand.

"Thank you so much for sharing our special day with us."

I hug Alana. I won't see her for the next couple of weeks while she and

Vinny are on their honeymoon in Europe.

"I can't believe you and Deven are an item," she whispers into my ear. "When I come back you have to tell me everything."

"I will. Enjoy your honeymoon." I smile at her, and give Vinny a quick hug.

Deven and I walk hand in hand out to the valet. He hands over the ticket to the valet, and pulls me aside.

"Did you have a good time?"

"I did. Did you?"

"I did as well only because I was here with you." He smiles at me and looks at me with content eyes.

"I'm going to miss her."

"She'll be back after her honeymoon."

"I know, but she's my lunch companion."

"Well, why don't I take her place while she's gone?"

"You will do that for me?"

"Of course I will. I'll have Catrina rearrange my schedule and keep lunch open for you." He runs his fingers along my jawline. "You know I will do anything for you." *Swoon.* Deven Blake is my Prince Charming.

The valet pulls up in Deven's car.

"Nice car sir," the valet says to Deven.

"Thank you," Deven says and slips the valet a tip. Deven opens the door for me, and I climb in taking care not to damage my dress.

Deven held my hand the entire drive back to his penthouse. As soon as we're in his penthouse he takes me into his arms and seals his mouth over mine. *Hmm.* He threads his fingers with mine, and leads me to his bedroom.

I tug on his tie and pull him closer to me. Giving him a seductive smile, I unknot his tie, slide it off his neck, and fling it on the floor. He removes his cufflinks and places it on the dresser. Gazing lovingly into each other's eyes, my fingers work on unbuttoning his shirt. I push his shirt off of his shoulders, and run my hands down his hard chest before unhooking his pants.

"You're stunning," he says kissing me.

I ask him to unzip my dress, and turn around. His hands work quickly to unzip it letting it pool at my feet. Then he spins me back around.

"You are absolutely divine," he says devouring me with his eyes as I stand there semi-naked. He kneels down. His fingers slowly travel down the length of my body making me burn with desire. His hands grasp my hips, and he kisses my belly. Inch by inch he slides my panties down leaving me exposed there. He trails his nose down to my private area and nestles his nose there. Ohmigod! He drops a kiss at the top of my mound, and rises to his feet. I look at him and his expression completely unravels me as the air between us sizzles. He pushes my hair back, and lifts me up. He puts me down on his enormous bed. We continue to kiss while his fingers find my wet spot.

"Fuck angel. You're so ready."

He climbs onto the bed, and immediately sinks himself into me. He moves and rocks me with him. My hands grip his muscular back and my legs tighten around his hips while he buries himself deep inside of me. I arch my back and cry out in pleasure. He hooks an arm around my hips and fluidly rolls me onto him. I slowly sit up so that I am straddling him. Why am I suddenly feeling shy? What am I supposed to do now? He firmly grips my waist and holds my eyes.

"It will come naturally. Follow my lead, okay?"

He lifts his hips and move up and down until we are both in rhythm. I throw my head back as I take over control, and quicken my pace.

"That's it angel. Ride me hard baby."

And I do. I ride him hard like he wants. We are both lost to the passion and lust consuming us. He plunges into me and shatters my world. Oh my, oh my, oh my! I collapse onto his chest still trembling from the intensity of my orgasm. He wraps his arms around me. Bodies slick with sweat, we embrace each other tightly as we struggle to catch our breaths.

"That was fucking amazing angel." He kisses my hair.

We slide under the covers, and he turns off the lights. His strong arms come around me and I fall asleep in the arms of the man that completely owns me.

CHAPTER THIRTY

November

CARI

The crisp cool autumn air has set in, and the leaves have started to fall off the trees. November brought along colder temperatures, and my six month review. It is no secret Myra is not a kind soul when it comes down to reviews. Though Myra is still the Ice Queen, she's become a little bit more tolerable which I suspect has to do with the fact that I'm seeing Deven. I held my breath the entire time Myra went over my performance with me. Surprisingly my review was not a disappointing one.

When I get back to my desk there are a dozen or so emails from Deven. Most of them asking how my review with Myra went. I read each one, but the last one peaks my interest. I reread the email.

> Cari,
> My half-siblings are in New York. How does dinner on Saturday sound? See if Rodrigo and Hunter can join.
> Yours forever,
> Deven

His half-siblings are still somewhat of a mystery to me, and I would like to meet them especially since Deven loves them.

> Deven,
> I'd love to meet your half-siblings.

Dinner on Saturday is perfect. I'll check
with R and H.
Forever yours,
Cari

~ * ~

Deven made reservations at a fancy French restaurant on the upper West Side. He was insistent that Mauricio pick us up and drive us to the restaurant, but I managed to convince him that it would just be easier to meet there.

Rodrigo whistles when he sees me. "Damn girl! You must be Deven's main course."

"I want to make a nice impression on his half-siblings."

"You always look fantastic thanks to me. After all, was it not I who showed you how to dress up?"

"Yes, and thank you."

"Oh, you're welcome sweetie." He straightens his tie. "Now how do I look?"

"You look dashing."

"I do, don't I?" He smiles at his reflection in the mirror. "I wish Hunter was feeling better so he could come with us."

"Me too."

"Shall we go gorgeous?"

I reach for my bag. "Yeah. Let's do this."

"Come on then."

We hail a cab and are on our way to the restaurant. I'm fiddling with my dress.

Rodrigo grabs my hand. "Stop fidgeting."

"What if they don't like me?"

"Sweetie, you're not dating them. You're dating their half-brother who happens to be hot, and in love with you."

Sometimes I think Rodrigo forgets that I'm nothing like him. My making a good impression means everything to me. And since Deven is the first guy I have been with in years it's important to me that his family likes me. Deven's family means a lot to him and if his half-siblings do not like me I do not want to be the wedge that comes between them.

Traffic is light and we make it to the restaurant five minutes early. My gorgeous boyfriend has already arrived and is waiting at the entrance for us. He kisses me on the cheek and tells me how beautiful I look. He shakes Rodrigo's hand, and leads us to the private dining room. *Breathe Cari. Breathe.* Mayleen is sandwiched between the half-siblings. As we approach the table, Deven's half-brother gets up from his seat.

"Ken. Kaitlin. This is Cari," Deven says introducing us.

Ken is handsome with brown hair, hazel eyes, and a slightly hooked nose. He shakes my hand and then gives me a cheek to cheek kiss. "Nice to finally meet the beautiful lady who Deven talks about constantly."

His comment makes some color creep to my cheeks. "It's nice to meet you as well."

Kaitlin is about my height with a pixie cut that suits her heart shaped face. Like Ken, she has matching hazel eyes, and a matching hooked nose. Kaitlin on the other hand is not as friendly as Ken is. She doesn't make a move to shake my hand until Deven tells her to. I don't think she likes me.

Deven introduces Rodrigo and they exchange polite greetings before we all take our seats. The server comes over and pops open the bottle of Armand de Brignac that is sitting in the ice bucket, and pours it into our glasses. Deven takes away May's glass.

"Deven, can't I have a sip?" Mayleen asks.

"Absolutely not," Deven responds.

Mayleen pouts.

"You're not missing out on anything May," Kaitlin chimes in.

"Then Deven should let me have a sip."

"You're not twenty-one yet, and I am responsible for you when you are with me; therefore, you follow the rules."

Mayleen rolls her eyes.

"So you both met at BG?" Kaitlin asks, but there seems to be contempt in her voice.

I am about to reply, but Deven beats me to it. "I first met Cari at a club

135

before I even knew who she was and where she was working." He turns to look at me and takes my hand under the table giving it a squeeze.

"Huh." Kaitlin turns to me. "Guess you're more than just a fling. He doesn't believe in dating anyone that works for him."

"Shut up Kait," Ken says.

"She's the exception," Deven says sounding quite annoyed at Kaitlin.

"Enough Kaitie. Don't ruin tonight," Ken says.

Kaitlin's jaw tightens, and she takes a big swallow of her champagne refusing to make eye contact with any one of us.

The dinner passes by quickly, and smoothly. I talk mostly to Rodrigo and Ken. Ken is attentive, empathetic, and intelligent. His qualities almost mirror Deven's. He will make a great teacher. Kaitlin prefers to talk to Deven and Mayleen instead, making me feel like a pariah. When we said our goodbyes, Ken embraces me, but Kaitlin just waves without saying a word.

~ * ~

I lift the duvet cover and slide in next to Deven.

"Give me one minute baby doll." He finishes up whatever he was doing, and places the iPad on the nightstand. He removes his eyeglasses and sets them on top of the iPad. I love when he wears his glasses. What is it about men and glasses? He turns off the lights, and lies on his side facing me.

"You're so beautiful."

"You say that a lot."

"Because it's true." He strokes my cheek as I splay my hand on his chiseled chest.

We have not discussed the dinner at all, but I have to know what Kaitlin's beef is with me.

"I think your brother likes me, but I'm not so sure about Kaitlin."

"Ken better remember you're mine. As for Kait, she has some issues."

"With me?"

"No. She's had some complicated issues the past few years which I don't want to get into. And she's mad at me anyhow."

"Why is she mad at you?"

"She's not happy I'm seeing you. She's been trying to get me to hook up with her best friend."

It all made sense now. Kaitlin will never like me as long as I'm with Deven. This is the thing I had been dreading.

"Oh?"

"Her best friend has always had a crush on me, but I don't feel the same about her."

I should feel better after he just admitted he has no feelings for Kaitlin's best friend, but I don't. I don't want to be the cause of a family rift.

"Don't worry about Kaitlin. She'll eventually come around."

"Deven?"

"Yes, angel?"

"Why do you never speak of your mother?"

"I do speak of her."

"No, I meant your biological mother."

He doesn't say anything and instead rolls onto his back. He never talks about his biological mother, and I wonder why. The only thing I know is that she's been married four times. He puts his hands behind his head.

"When I was six, I caught my mom in bed with another man. She never knew I witnessed it. A few months later, she told my father she was leaving him and wanted a divorce. She accused him of not having any time for her. Can you believe that? I wish he had known she was cheating on him. I remember how hurt my father was. He worked hard to build his business to try to give his family a good life, but she didn't want an absentee husband, or so she said. Not even a year after their divorce was final, she remarried.

"Around the time she left my father, she was pregnant with baby number two and chose to have an abortion. My father tried to convince her to stay, to keep the baby…that they can try to make it work and be a family, but she would hear nothing of it. She robbed my father of another child, and me of a sibling. No matter what my father may have thought, she never loved him. She was just a gold digging whore."

I flinch at his harsh words.

"I apologize for speaking in such manner about her, but she's all about money and status."

"You said you didn't speak to her often."

"No, I don't. During the separation and after the divorce, my father made me speak to her every other day. As I got older, the need to speak to her became less and less. During my high school and college years, she only called me on holidays and my birthday. Now that I'm running the company she wants to speak to me all the time...acting like the concerned mother she should have been."

"Sometimes as people get older they have a change of heart. They may regret their past actions and look to make things right again."

"No. She wants to make sure I will keep her financially happy in the event my father dies, or her current husband stops providing for her. She needs money in her life. It's her number one love – not her children."

I don't know what it's like to have a mother, but Grams sure did a good job being both a mother and grandmother to me. Every child wants their parents love. Deven wanted his mother's love and never received it in the way he should have. I understand now why he loves Leigh. She is the mother he never had.

"I wish it was different for you."

"It doesn't matter. Let's not talk about her anymore. I rather concentrate on making love to you."

Oh, for God's sake.

"We can't. It's that time of month."

He sighs. "Damn it. Well then let me hold you."

I happily oblige.

CHAPTER THIRTY-ONE

December

CARI

You know that song "It's the Most Wonderful Time of the Year"? Well, it surely is in New York City with the stores and streets decorated for the holidays while shoppers flood the streets of Manhattan with hands full of shopping bags.

The company's annual holiday party is at a waterfront restaurant overlooking the East River. The employees are permitted to bring along a guest so I decided to bring Rodrigo as my guest.

Rodrigo looks dapper in his brand new Hugo Boss suit he purchased when we went shopping for tonight's party. I opted for the sale rack and found a simple strapless black lace cocktail dress with an ivory satin sash. What I saved on the dress I ended up splurging on my new Manolo Blahnik pumps.

Rodrigo and I are both awestruck when we arrive. The restaurant has been transformed to resemble a winter wonderland. The white décor and illuminated blue lights gives the room a cool feeling. Silver Christmas trees grace the room, and snowflakes and stars hang from the ceiling. A sleigh filled with presents rests in a corner, and each table has centerpieces of white tree branches with snow birds on them. A live band plays holiday music as the employees and guests mingle. Alana and her husband are by the bar.

"I've never seen anything like this," Rodrigo says as he records video footage of the decorated restaurant on his phone.

"This is much nicer than last year's set up. I think they outdid themselves this year," Alana says.

"The company really knows how to make an impression," adds Vinny.

I scan the room for Deven.

"Looking for your boyfriend?" Alana asks.

"Am I that obvious?"

"Yes, but I can't blame you. You have to watch for some of the piranhas here."

I spot Deven talking to someone.

"Rodrigo, Deven's over there. I want to let him know we're here."

"I'm going with you."

"Excuse us Alana. We'll catch up with you in a few."

"Yeah, of course. We'll talk later."

Rodrigo and I make our way over to Deven. He is speaking to one of the office girls who has on a mini dress with a very low V-neck cut in the front. Her breasts are all but popping out of her dress. She laughs at something he says, and plants her hand on my boyfriend's forearm.

"Who's that skank that has her hand on your man?"

"I can't remember her name."

"And what's with that dress? It screams 'hoe'. Does she know this is a holiday party?"

I watch as she bats her eyes at Deven, and laughs at whatever it is he is telling her.

"I think you need to remind her that he's taken."

I don't like the feeling of being jealous, and try hard to keep this emotion at bay.

"I can tell it's bothering you that she is touching him. "

"It does, but what can I say or do without sounding like an insecure girlfriend?"

"If roles were reversed, do you think Deven would put up with some guy speaking to you and touching you?"

"I know he wouldn't."

"You're right. He would go insane with jealousy. I'll handle this. Watch me." He strides up to Deven and I follow behind.

Rodrigo calls out Deven's name and he turns around. I blink. He is so devastatingly handsome. He sees me and comes to me forcing office girl to drop her hand. He leans in to give me a kiss me on the cheek.

"Cari, you take my breath away," Deven says gazing at me like a lovesick schoolboy.

"That's a nice dress," office girl says curling her lips into a fake smile. Why is she following him?

"Rodrigo, how are you?" Deven shakes his hand.

"I'm well. I think Cari is by far the most beautiful here tonight. Don't you agree Deven?" Rodrigo asks.

"Yes, she is. She always is."

My cheeks flush instantly.

"There are lots of beautiful women here tonight," office girl says sounding deflated by Deven's response.

"I don't think so," Rodrigo says and gives office girl a bitch stare. *Oh my God.* I need to drag Rodrigo away before he gets another word in, and bitch slaps her. I know what my best friend is like and he will be the bigger bitch at the end.

"Rodrigo, I would like a drink. Come with me to the bar."

"I'll be more than happy to accompany you. Why don't I go with you?" Deven offers me his arm, and I take it.

"Coming Rodrigo?"

"You know what? I just remembered I had to ask Alana something. I'll look for her and catch up with you two at the bar."

"It was nice chatting with you Janice," Deven says and pulls me away. Janice is her name. Ta-ta Janice.

"You really do look beautiful Cari."

"Thank you."

On our way to the bar he is stopped by a few of the employees wishing to say hi to him and make small talk. Deven's interaction with his entire staff is amazing. He knows each and every one of his employees and gives them his undivided attention except for maybe the few employees that get under his skin like Jeremy. When we finally make it to the bar, he asks me what I would like. The bartender sees Deven and immediately takes his order.

"Here babe." He hands me my cranberry and vodka.

"Thank you." I take a sip of the refreshing liquor.

The emcee welcomes everyone to tonight's party and invites everyone onto the dance floor. Deven is an excellent dancer and pulls me to the dance floor with him. We dance a couple of songs together before being interrupted.

"I'm sorry to interrupt Deven," Lilah says. *Yeah, right.* "We need to get on stage now."

Deven looks down at his watch. "Yeah, I guess it is time."

Lilah makes no attempt to move and stands beside us waiting for Deven to go with her.

"Why don't you start? I'll be there in a couple of minutes," Deven says.

"Sure." She throws me a nasty look and stalks away.

"I'm sorry baby. I've got to do my speech and the presentations."

"I understand. Go do what you need to do."

"Okay, but don't disappear on me."

"I won't. I promise."

I watch him walk over to the stage. Lilah immediately flashes a smile and puts her hand over his. I want to run over there and tell her to get her filthy paws off my man, but I just don't have the courage to do so.

"Seriously? Another skank touching your man?" Rodrigo asks.

"That's Lilah." Lilah bends down and my mouth drops open. Her breasts are about to pop out of her dress.

"Oh, so that's Lilah. Does she know what double sided tape is?" Rodrigo asks.

"I don't think so. Maybe I'll mail her some."

"Good idea. If I'm going to hang around for a women strip show, I'm going to need another drink."

Rodrigo and I go to the bar and order another drink. I am going to need something stronger to make it through the night of piranhas surrounding Deven.

CHAPTER THIRTY-TWO

DEVEN

A couple of days after the holiday party I went back to Los Angeles to oversee the opening of our new offices. Now I am back home and hitting the busy mall with Cari to finish our Christmas shopping. I completed my shopping for Cari prior to the L.A. trip. I catch Cari stealing a glance at me so I draw her closer to me and kiss her.

"What was that for?"

"Because I love you."

She gives a coy smile. "I love you too." I love hearing her tell me she loves me.

"I know just what to get Esmeralda," she says as we stop in front of Gucci.

My phone rings. I look to see who is calling. Ugh! It's Rochelle. I ignore the call, and go into the store with Cari. My phone rings again, and I see it's Rochelle again. I ignore it. Cari picks out a wallet and then looks at the handbags. She asks to see one, and puts it on her shoulder looking at her reflection in the mirror.

"You like that bag?"

"Yes."

"It's yours. It's my gift to you."

"You already bought a bag for me when you were in Hong Kong. I can buy myself a bag."

"I know you can, but why would you when your rich boyfriend wants to buy it for you?"

"I don't want you to spoil me."

I love spoiling her. She deserves everything my money can buy for her. She's the only person I have ever wanted to spoil, and she doesn't even want to be spoiled. I lean into her ear. "I want to spoil you. You need to start getting used to it."

She sighs and concedes. Again my phone rings. Rochelle's name appears on the screen again. I reach for my wallet and pull out my credit card.

"Cari, I've got to make a call. Here is my credit card. Use it." I lean into her ear again and whisper. "If you don't, I won't make love to you for a week." Okay, that was a really stupid thing for me to say. As if I could actually last that long without having her. She takes the credit card from my hand pleasing me.

"Thank you." I kiss her temple and leave the store to return Rochelle's call.

"Hellooo," she slurs on the other end. Great, she's drunk.

"I hope this is important and about Kait."

"I – I wanted to know when you were coming back to L.A."

"Why?"

"I miss you."

"Don't start Rochelle. You're drunk."

"I am not! Why are you being so rude Dev baby?"

"What is wrong with you Rochelle? You act like I'm your boyfriend."

"Aren't you?"

"Rochelle, I need for you to stop this. I'm off the market. You know damn well I'm seeing someone so do me a favor and don't call me unless it's an emergency regarding Kait." I hang up.

I know I was a being a complete asshole, but I had to put a stop to her random calls especially when she was in her inebriated state. As I head back to the store I get a text from Kaitlin. For Christ's sake! Rochelle called her crying about how I rejected her. Rochelle is being a damn drama queen right now and my sister is buying into this shit. Of course she would. Lesson learned. Never fuck your sister's best friend because it will come back to you.

Just a few feet outside of Gucci I see Cari talking to a guy. Who the hell is he? It's only when I get closer do I notice Cari's face is ashen. I immediately go to her and put a protective arm around her.

"What's going on here?"

The guy sizes me up. "Introduce us Cari," the asshole says.

I narrow my eyes at him. "And who might you be?"

"I might ask you the same thing."

I have to fight the urge to punch the shit out of this motherfucker. "I asked you first."

He looks at Cari. "You didn't tell him about our past?"

I turn to Cari, and see nothing but fear on her face. What the fuck did he do to her?

The asshole's finger touches the bottom of Cari's chin and she flinches. I drop the arm I have around Cari and take a step forward.

"Keep your hands off of her."

"Whatcha gonna do if I don't?"

"Listen pal, and listen carefully. I know a lot of people. Lawyers, politicians, judges, cops, and FBI to name a few. I will not hesitate to use my powers and connections to throw your motherfucking ass in jail."

"Psh," he says and laughs it off. "They have no reason to put me in jail."

I had to do something to scare him. I lean into the guy and whisper. "I know what you did to her and the statute of limitations has not yet run out." The guy's face pales and he takes a step back. "Leave now, or I will call the cops." I pull my cell phone out of my pocket to make it look like I'm not bluffing. I don't know what he did to Cari, but whatever it was he will not get away with it. The motherfucker walks away without another word. I pull a shaking Cari into my arms. She buries her face in my chest.

"Let's get out of here," I tell her.

I guide her out of the mall and drive back home. She's been quiet since she's run into him. I try to get her to tell me what she got me for Christmas, but she just gives me a half smile. Once we're home, I take her into the living room. She sits down on the couch holding a pillow to her. I sit down beside her.

"Do you want to talk about it?"

"I'm sorry Deven."

I hope she is not apologizing for that asshole. "I'm not sure what you are apologizing for."

"For the incident at the mall."

"With that motherfucker? No need to." I lean forward with my elbows on my knees. "I do want to know who he is." I have a hunch he may be a past boyfriend, but I need to hear it from her.

She brings her legs up to the couch tucking them under her. She nervously pushes her hair behind her ear. "He's my ex-boyfriend."

Her ex-boyfriend? What the hell did she even see in him?

"You were quite pale when I got to you. Did something happen?"

She doesn't answer immediately. "When we first went out, he was charming and sweet."

I find that hard to believe, and let out a snort.

"What?"

"I don't believe he possesses any of those traits."

"He did. We started seeing each other when I was a freshman in college, and he was a senior. There was a project in one of my classes and I was paired up with a guy, and my ex was not happy about the arrangement. There had been some scheduling conflicts between my project partner and I, and a couple of times we stayed late at the library to work on the project. I chose not to tell my ex about it because I knew it would only upset him, but he found out anyway. And when he did he snapped."

"What exactly happened when he snapped?" I brace myself for whatever she is about to reveal to me.

"First he called me names...slut, whore, cunt. Then he hit me. I had a black eye and bruises all over my body."

Oh, God. I wish I had punched that asshole when I had the chance to. What kind of monster is he for hitting her? My hands fist. I close my eyes and count to ten to calm myself.

"That was the first time."

My eyes shot wide open. "What?" I can barely contain the anger in my voice. "First time?"

"Whenever I did something he did not like he would hit me."

"How long was he abusing you?"

"A while."

"What is a while?"

"For months."

I pinch the bridge of my nose, and inhale a deep breath. "Please tell me you pressed charges against the motherfucker."

Cari shakes her head. I don't believe she let that fucking bastard escape punishment.

"Why not?"

"I didn't want anyone to know what happened. It was so shameful."

"But he is still walking around freely! What if he abuses other women as well?"

Cari bites her lower lip. I can tell she's never given that any thought.

She rubs her eyes. "I know. Rodrigo said the same thing to me, but I just couldn't do it."

"You can probably still press charges for the abuse. I will speak with my lawyer."

She shakes her head vehemently. "No! You can't. It doesn't matter. Other than today, I have not had any run-ins with him."

I love her and I will do everything in my power to protect her. If that motherfucker ever comes near Cari again, his balls will be served to him on a dinner plate.

"Tell me what his name is."

"Everett Winthrop."

I file that name away in my head. I will have my security team dig for information on him. He's going to get what he deserves.

"There's something else I haven't told you."

There's more? This asshole is really going to get it. "What is it?"

"He forced me to have sex with him."

A rage of fury sweeps over me. "He raped you?"

She nods. I pound my fist on the coffee table rattling the contents on it.

"Were you a virgin when he raped you?"

"Yes," she says very softly. The fucking asshole took what wasn't his to take.

I have a feeling I know the answer to my next question, but I have to ask. "Did you have him incarcerated for the rape?"

"No."

"You need to press charges against that motherfucker Cari."

"No! I can't."

"Why the fuck not? I am almost certain you are within the statute of limitations. I'm going to ask my lawyer."

"Please don't Deven."

"Cari, he raped you! He had no fucking right to do that! That's a crime. He should be behind bars for it. You are letting him get away with what he did to you."

"I don't ever want it to go to trial. I don't want to relive it. Not any bit of it. Please don't make me relive that again. Please." She covers her face with her hands and cries into them.

I hold her tightly to me. "What he did to you was unacceptable." I rub her back. "I know this is hard for you, but it makes me so angry that he thought he had the right to hit you, and rape you."

"Stop Deven. Just let it be."

I pull back. "Let it be? He doesn't deserve a place on this planet. He deserves to be locked up."

She looks at me with wet, pleading eyes. "You don't understand. It took years of counseling for me to finally overcome it. I had a fear of dating again despite my therapist urging me to try. It's taken me this long to let myself date again. You are the first guy I have been with since Everett. I don't ask for much so please just let it go so I can continue to live my life."

As much as I do not want to let this go, I give in to her imploring. "If that's what you want. But Cari, if that motherfucker comes within one millimeter of you I will have him thrown in jail."

She nods. "Thank you, but I don't think he will ever come near me again."

"He better not because I meant what I said." I envelope her in my arms again, and kiss her hair. It fucking kills me to know someone could hurt her. "I will never ever mistreat you. You're safe with me."

She holds me tightly. "I know."

I wish Cari would change her mind and let me consult my lawyer. I would love nothing more than to see that asshole arrested, tried, and locked up for good. He needs to feel the pain and shame he put Cari through. He better watch himself because karma can be a real bitch.

CHAPTER THIRTY-THREE

CARI

I never wanted Deven to know about Everett nor what he did to me. I was afraid he would be ashamed of me and want nothing more to do with me. Who wants damaged goods anyhow? But Deven proved me wrong. He loves me, and didn't walk away. He stayed with me.

With Christmas being less than a week away, everyone in the office is hustling and bustling to finish up their work before the office closes for the next couple of weeks.

I take a longer than usual lunch break today with Alana as Myra started her vacation early. After lunch, I head into the restroom. I had just gone into one of the stalls when I hear someone enter the ladies room. There's some chatting and I realize there are at least two ladies here. Deven's name comes up in their conversation, and I keep still so I can listen in. Thank God the walls of these stalls stretch from the ceiling to the floor so no one knows I'm even here.

"I can't believe he is still with her. She must be after his money," voice one says.

I recognize that voice. That's Lilah out there. Why is she saying such horrible things about me?

"Why does it matter? It's not like he's going to get back together with you," voice two says.

"How can you be so sure he won't want me back? We do have a history you know."

"Sure, but that's in the past. If he wanted you back it would have already happened." I silently cheer on voice two. "Maybe he just isn't interested in you anymore."

There's a stretch of silence before Lilah speaks. "Can you keep a secret?"

"Of course I can."

"We almost had a baby together."

I cover my mouth. *What? He impregnated her?*

"Almost?"

"I had a miscarriage."

"Lilah, I'm sorry to hear. But you do know that does not mean he's still interested in you."

"I think there's a part of him that still wants me. Why would he keep me here if he didn't feel anything for me?"

"I can't answer that hon."

"I'm working on making him see we belong together."

"Even though he is seeing that girl?"

Lilah laughs. "She won't last. Myra has a reputation for running her assistants out. "

"That's true." They both laugh.

"Let's go. I have to be at a meeting in five minutes."

I hear them leave, but I can't move. I lean against the wall feeling nauseous. Though it happened in the past, and I should let it go, it still hurt to hear that Deven got Lilah pregnant.

Concentrating on my work the remainder of the day proved to be challenging, and I'm relieved when the work day comes to an end. My cell phone rings again as I gather my belongings. Deven's name pops up on the caller ID. He's been trying to reach me since I returned from lunch, but I ignore it like I have done all afternoon. I'm not ready to talk to him.

~ * ~

DEVEN

Cari has not replied to any of my emails, texts, or calls. The lack of response from her has me concerned. It's half past five. Locking up my office I go over to check on her. Her back is to me. I clear my throat to get her attention. She whirls around and looks at me, and then turns her back to me again. What the hell was that about?

"I have been worried about you. Mind telling me why you have not responded to me?"

"It's been a busy day." She snaps back. I raise my eyebrows. Is it that time of month?

"Are you ready to go then?"

She tries to step around me, but I'm quick and grab her hand. I turn and face her. Her eyes are glistening with tears. No, definitely not that time of month.

"What's the matter Cari?"

She looks away from me. "Everything is fine."

Nuh-uh. I don't buy it. "Something is wrong. What is going on?"

"Nothing."

"You cannot tell a lie. Tell me what it is so I can help you."

"I don't want to talk about it. I'm going home."

"All right. Let's go then."

"No. I mean I'm going home to my apartment."

What the fuck? "Why?"

"Because that's *my* home."

"Your home is also with me."

"No, that's your home."

I place my hands on her shoulders. "No, that's *our* home. The home is ours Cari. Now enough of this. You are going to go back home with me, and we are going to sit down and talk like sensible adults. You seem to be out of sorts." I run my fingers down her cheek. "I want you to talk to me." She closes her eyes and acquiesces to me.

~ * ~

"Why don't you go get comfortable and I'll whip up something for dinner?"

She gives me a nod and goes to the bedroom. I search the refrigerator to see what I have. There's a package of chicken. I sauté the chicken and toss it up with vegetables and a cream sauce. As I set the table, Cari comes in wearing a tight shirt and pants. *I rather have her for dinner.*

"Perfect timing love."

We both take our seats, and eat in uncomfortable silence. I don't like this kind of silence. She's hardly spoken to me and has tried to keep her distance from me all night. She finishes her dinner first.

"A little bit hungry?"

She smiles sheepishly. "Yes. Thank you for making dinner."

"It's my pleasure. Why don't you go into the living room and relax? Let me clean up and then we'll talk." I take the plates and silverware to the sink.

"I'll help you." She seems a little better now that she's eaten. I hope it stays this way.

"Whatever you'd like baby doll."

I bring our wine glasses to the living room after the kitchen is cleaned up. I sit on the couch and she sits on the further end of the couch. Jesus Christ. This has got to stop now.

"What's going on? You seem to be mad at me, but I'm not sure why."

She stares down at her nails. "Why didn't you tell me that Lilah was pregnant with your baby?"

How did she know about that? If that bitch said something to Cari I will fire her.

I narrow my eyes at her. "How did you know she was pregnant?"

"Oh, God. So, it is true."

"Before you start thinking the worst, let me explain." I run my hands down my face. "Lilah was pregnant, but it was not my baby. We had already started to drift apart, or at least I started to. She cheated on me and pretended it was my baby so she could keep her hold on me. The baby was conceived during a time I was not even on campus. When I learned how far along she was, I did the math, and knew there was no possibility it could be mine. She had been cheating on me for some time. After she lost the baby I confronted her about the cheating and that I knew I was not the father. She had the fucking audacity to lie in my face and deny all of it. It was what I needed to end our relationship."

"You should have told me about this Deven."

She did not just go there. "And you should have told me about Everett. I was not deliberately keeping it from you. The baby was never mine so there was no point in bringing it up. All that is in the past and I'm not living in the past. I'm focused on my future. A future which includes you."

Her eyes are glassy and I scoot over and reach for her hands. She doesn't pull them away and that's a good thing. I can't have Lilah cause Cari anymore heartache.

"You are the world to me Cari, and I don't want that part of my past to fuse with our future." Doesn't she see how much she means to me?

"I just don't want any more surprises."

"There are no more surprises." I raise her hand to my lips and place a kiss on it.

The only surprise is when I fire Lilah on Monday.

CHAPTER THIRTY-FOUR

CARI

This is the first Christmas in a long time that I actually look forward to celebrating. Hunter, and I spent Christmas Eve with the Sanchezes at their house. We are spending the morning with Rodrigo's family, and then going to the Blake Estate later for Christmas dinner. After breakfast we gather in the family room to exchange presents. Rodrigo hands me an envelope.

"What's this?"

"Go ahead and open it before I spoil the surprise and tell you."

I open the envelope. Wow! It's a three hundred dollar gift card to Saks Fifth Avenue.

"Rodrigo, this is way too much."

"It's just a little something sweetie. Merry Christmas Cari."

"Thank you. You have to go shopping with me though."

"Oh, absolutely honey. Did you think I wasn't?"

I laugh, and catch Hunter roll his eyes. Hunter despises shopping, and it's a trip I am certain he will not be making with us.

"I can't wait to see what Deven got you for Christmas. He probably got you something fancy," Rodrigo says.

"Probably. You think he will like what I got him?"

"Why wouldn't he?"

I shrug. "He has everything. I want my gift to stand out from what his ex-girlfriends gave him in the past."

"Who cares what his exes gave him? You have to stop feeling like you need to measure up to them. Let go of that insecurity," Rodrigo whispers. "You are Carilyn Snow, and Deven Blake loves Carilyn Snow."

Rodrigo is right. I have to stop letting his past affect us. *Semper ad meliora.*

"You deserve him. Don't compare yourself to those past hoes of his. You are nothing like them."

"You're right as always." I hug him again loving his honesty. "Love you."

"Love you too."

~ * ~

We arrive at the Blake Estate in two separate cars.

"Holy shit Cari! I thought you said their house is huge," Esmeralda says as Rodrigo parks the car.

"It is."

"This," she points to the house, "is like majorly huge. It's a mansion."

"Not according to Deven."

"Okay, whatever. Nice car," she says as her eyes fixate on the Jaguar.

"That belongs to Deven," Rodrigo chimes in.

"Seriously? You are so lucky Cari. You've got a hot guy who's smart and rich," Esmeralda says. "Every girl's dream."

"He's a keeper," Hunter says.

"For sure," Rodrigo agrees.

Yeah, Deven is the whole package...attractive, intelligent, wealthy, and generous. And best of all, he's mine.

The men grab the presents while Mrs. Sanchez, Esmeralda, and I walk up to the house. I ring the doorbell. Mayleen comes to the door and invites us in. She greets us with a big hug. After all the formal introductions are made, Deven makes his way down the staircase.

"Merry Christmas everyone." He approaches me first and kisses me on the cheek. He then moves on to greet everyone.

"Where should we put the presents?" Esmeralda asks.

"Mr. Sanchez, let me take that off your hands." Deven takes the bags of presents from Rodrigo's father. "Rodrigo and Hunter, would you mind giving me a hand?"

"Not at all." They help bring the remaining presents into the living room where a beautifully trimmed 15-foot Christmas tree stands. An abundance of presents lay underneath the tree. Leigh comes in and welcomes all of us. Leigh and Mayleen invite everyone into the kitchen for a drink before giving them a tour of their palatial home. Deven and I stay behind.

"You dazzle me as always." He places his hands on my neck and kisses me.

"Did you visit with your dad this morning?"

"I did."

"How is he?"

"It wasn't one of his better days. He was very quiet today. It's very discouraging to see him continue to deteriorate." Deven's eyes are watery. My heart sinks knowing what he is going through. My arms reach around his waist and I press my cheek to his chest holding him tightly to me. The doorbell rings causing us to pull apart.

"That must be Brad."

"I'll get it!" Mayleen shouts as she runs past us to open the front door. Deven scowls.

"What's the matter?"

"I think my sister has a crush on Brad."

"Is that a bad thing?"

"Yes, it is."

"Why?"

"He's much older than she is, and he's a player."

Mayleen brings Brad into the living room. They place the gifts Brad brought under the tree first.

"Merry Christmas Cari," Brad says and gives me a peck on the cheek.

"Merry Christmas Brad."

"And a Merry Christmas to you, boss."

Deven laughs and gives him a man hug. "Merry Christmas."

"Can I get you something to drink Brad?" Mayleen asks sweetly.

"I'm fine for now May. Thanks. Where's everyone?"

"On the tour," Deven replies.

"Mom's excited to have so many people here for Christmas," Mayleen says.

"I hope you're starving because she made a lot of food," Deven says.

"Always," Brad responds.

~ * ~

After an amazing dinner Leigh had made, we come together in the living room to talk, drink, and open presents. Deven and I sit together on the piano bench. Mayleen has the task of handing everyone their presents. Deven reaches under the tree for the Tiffany bag, and hands it to me.

My hands are trembling as I receive the bag. No one has ever bought me a gift from Tiffany's. I pull out the infamous blue box out of the bag and untie the red ribbon. *Holy cow.* My mouth hangs open when I see what is inside the velvet box…a shiny platinum necklace with a heart lock pendant encrusted in sparkling diamonds.

"If you don't like it, it can be exchanged for something else."

Not like it? Is he crazy? This is the most expensive and most beautiful present I have ever received. I grab hold of his hand. "No, this is beautiful. You shouldn't have spent so much money on my gift."

He brings my hand to his lips and kisses the back of it. "You're worth it angel. My heart belongs to you." He points to the heart pendant. "That represents my heart and only you have the key to it."

Gasp. Swoon. I look into his adoring eyes. "Oh Deven, it's so thoughtful. Thank you." Forgetting where I am for a minute I kiss him.

"Seriously? Can you two lovebirds stop that?" Brad asks.

"You're just jealous Wu. Wait until this happens to you. You'll understand then," Deven says.

"*If* it happens you mean."

I catch the frown on Mayleen's face. She does have a crush on Brad.

"I have something else for you," Deven says and hands me another present.

I tear away at the wrapping and open the box. *Oh my God.* I don't believe it. It's the bracelet that I looked at when we were in Newport. I take it out of the box.

"I can't believe you bought this for me."

"How could I not? I saw how much you wanted the bracelet."

I throw my arms around his neck. "You're too good to me."

"No, baby. It's the other way around."

I smile at this wonderful man beside me. He put the sunshine back into my heart. I love him so much. I give my gift to him, and like an impatient child, he rips apart the wrapping. It really was a challenge buying a present for someone who has everything.

He lets out a whistle. "This is perfect Cari." He takes out the Maurice Lacroix watch I bought him. If I could have afforded it, I would have purchased a Chopard for him instead. "I love it. Thank you angel."

"You're welcome."

When it was time to leave, I grab my overnight bag from Rodrigo's car. Deven takes it and puts it in the trunk of his Jaguar. Instead of going back with Rodrigo, I am going to stay with Deven the next couple of weeks. We all say our farewell and go our separate ways.

"This is the best Christmas I've had in a long time."

"Good."

"Your mom really went all out for dinner."

"She did, but she enjoyed it. She loves big gatherings. The more the merrier. It also helps her take her mind off of Dad for a bit."

"Thank you again for my gifts. You really shouldn't have spent so much on me."

"Nor you on me. Cari, the gifts are nothing compared to how I feel about you. And I said I wanted to spoil you, and I will."

"You don't have to."

"I didn't say I have to. *I want to.*"

I'm thankful that it's dark and he can't see my rosy cheeks. I am one lucky girl.

CHAPTER THIRTY-FIVE

February

CARI

January rolls by, and we're halfway through the winter season. The Blake Group acquired another property in Los Angeles a few months ago and construction has begun on the new luxury residential building. Deven sent a few of his management team to Los Angeles to monitor the construction, and begin work on the next project. Deven has a few more properties he is looking to obtain in L.A., and Seattle which means he will be making more frequent trips to the west coast. With his increased travel schedule, he is contemplating on creating a new position for me. A position allowing me to accompany him on the trips so we can be together.

Myra was one of the chosen to go to L.A. Her temporary reassignment left me with more responsibilities. I just completed the proposal for the lobby renovation in one of the residential buildings BG owns on the Upper West Side, and decide to hand it in to Deven today. I hardly see him during work hours as his days are usually full, but he did mention on the way in to work this morning that today is the first time in a very long time he has a clear schedule, and can catch up.

"Hi, Catrina."

Catrina seems surprised to see me. "Hi there Cari."

"Hey, I need to see Deven."

She looks away from me and starts to shuffle some papers on her desk. "He's in a meeting."

Now I am the one who is surprised. What meeting could he possibly be in? "Deven mentioned he had a clear schedule today."

"Yeah, um, something came up unexpectedly." Catrina purposely avoids eye contact with me.

"Oh."

"I'll let him know you stopped by and maybe you can come back later."

It feels like she is rushing me out of here, but I don't know why. My gut tells me something is not right and she's covering it up.

"Sure. Thanks Catrina." I spin around on my heels and start to walk away when I hear laughter coming from the corridor. Spinning right back around I see Deven with a beautiful blonde alongside of him as they share a laugh.

"Thank you for being so accommodating today. It really was great seeing you again. Promise that you will call me when you come back to L.A." She purrs out the last sentence as she rubs her hand up and down his bicep. I want to rip her claws off of him, but I can't seem to move.

Deven notices that I am standing there as does Blondie.

"Cari, what are you doing here?"

"I came by to give you the proposal for the eighty-fifth street lobby renovations. I completed it sooner than I thought."

"Excellent. I'll take a look at it."

Deven makes no effort to introduce me to Blondie. Instead he extends his hand and I shove the folder in it. He winces and I immediately feel awful for doing that. It was childish of me. I'm letting my emotions take control.

Blondie interrupts. "How impressive Deven." Is she patronizing me? "Looks like you have a star employee here."

"She's much more than that." *Take that Blondie.* "Thank you Cari. I'd like to go over this with you."

"Of course. Give me a call, or send an email to me when you are ready to meet with me."

"I want to meet with you now."

I purse my lips. "Yes, sir."

That's Blondie's cue to leave and thankfully she does, but not before giving my boyfriend a kiss on the cheek leaving her lipstick on him. Deven steps aside to let me into his office first. He shuts the door behind him and sits in the chair next to me.

"Who was that?"

"That was Rochelle."

"Rochelle?" The name sounds familiar, but I do not recall where I have heard her name before.

"She's Kaitlin's best friend."

Oh God. Yes, she's the one who has a crush on him. The one his half-sister wants him to be with. Crap. She's gorgeous. How is it he's not with her instead?

"What was she doing here?"

"She came to audition for a role in a Broadway show. She's leaving tomorrow morning and just dropped by to say hi."

Sure she did.

"She left her lipstick on your cheek."

He reaches over his desk for a tissue, and scrubs it off his cheek.

"She was touching you like she has some kind of claim on you."

"She has no claim on me. You are the only one who has a claim on me. She's only a friend, and nothing more."

I feel like a fool. I hate that I am behaving like a jealous girlfriend.

"I'm sorry Deven. It's just that when she touched you and looked at you it just made me...it made me..." What is wrong with me? The words seem to be lodged in my throat.

"It made you feel jealous?" I nod. "You have nothing to worry about. There will always be some girl who has a crush on me." Is that supposed to make me feel better? "Know that my heart belongs to you, and only you. Come here."

I look into his serene blue eyes and see nothing but love and adoration. He pulls me onto his lap with an arm around my back. I lay my head on his shoulder, and let him hold me. For now I let go of my insecurity and all is right.

CHAPTER THIRTY-SIX

CARI

Deven and I celebrated Valentine's Day last weekend. He surprised me with a romantic weekend trip to Kiawah Island, and in addition gave me a fetching ruby and diamond bracelet. There really is no end to him spoiling me. He booked one of the elegant suites at The Sanctuary Hotel, and we spent most of our time in the bedroom on the beautiful four poster bed doing…well, you know. When we did manage to get dressed and venture out, we did a little bit of biking, sightseeing, and shopping. It was one of the best weekends ever.

Upon returning to New York from our blissful trip, Deven was informed that his Executive Assistant in the Los Angeles office had walked off the job. With her sudden departure he had to make arrangements to go out to L.A. to pick up the slack, and hire a replacement. There is no indication on how long he will have to be out there, and it leads to an incredible week of passionate sex before he had to leave the following Monday.

While Deven is in California, I stay in Chelsea with Rodrigo. Rodrigo and I have been talking about adding blond highlights to our hair for the longest time, so Rodrigo finally booked appointments for us to have it done today. I'm stoked as this will be the first drastic change I have done to my hair. We're sitting in our chairs waiting for the dye to set in. Rodrigo is looking at something on his phone while I watch the morning news. He mutters some profanity in Spanish, and I see him shaking his head with a hand over his eyes.

"Rodrigo, what's wrong?"

He uncovers his eyes and looks at me. "You need to see this."

"See what?"

He hands his cell phone over to me. I look at it and it's a tweet from one of those celebrity TV shows. *No! It can't be.* On the screen is a picture of Deven entering a restaurant with Rochelle. They are smiling at each other like a loving couple, and his hand is on her right hip. I read the caption below.

> *"Eligible bachelor and real estate mogul Deven Blake was spotted entering Chateau Marmont with actress Rochelle Fabian. Could the couple be rekindling their relationship?"*

Each word of the last sentence stabs me deep in the heart. He told me he had no interest in her, but he never told me they were in a relationship. I hand the phone back to Rodrigo.

"Don't believe everything you read. The writer obviously did not do his homework. These people will write any bullshit to make a buck."

"I know that," I snap at him unintentionally. *But there must be some truth to the story.*

"Hey, are you okay?"

I fight the urge to cry and look away. I will not let him see my teary eyes.

"Oh no girl. Don't go there." Sometimes I hate that he knows me so well. "That was probably not a date, and I'm sure he has a good explanation."

"Like what? That he needed a booty call?" I cross my arms.

Rodrigo cocks an eyebrow at my response. I cover my face. "These exes of his are really bringing out a different side of me."

"Look, you need to ask him if there is any truth to that story. If I find out that he hurt you again, I will brand his balls with a hot cast iron."

I scrunch my face, and then let out a sigh. "She's gorgeous Rodrigo. Sometimes I wonder why he isn't with her instead."

"Seriously? You're going to start this again? She's more like a plastic

Barbie doll with major surgical enhancements. You, on the other hand my dear, are beautiful, genuine, and real. You don't need to surgically enhance anything because you're perfect. Some people are just born beautiful inside and out, and you're one of them. You turn men's heads all the time – even the gay ones!"

"No. Look at me. I'm nothing like those girls he's been with. They're all gorgeous, voluptuous, and more experienced." I let my voice drop down to a whisper on the last word.

"Ha!" Rodrigo exclaims loudly capturing everyone's attention in the salon. He looks around the salon. "What is everyone looking at? Carry on about your business please."

I laugh as I see some of the customers mouths drop open at what he just said, but resume what they were doing before anyhow.

"You are all of that too. You have real boobs and a real ass. Leave all that self-doubt, and low self-esteem behind."

"I need to work on it."

"Yes, you do. You've grown up Cari darling. Insecurity is a thing of the past. Don't let it interfere with the good life you have right now."

"I'll try. You always know what to say to make me feel better. Thank you."

"Hey, that's what gay brothers are for."

CHAPTER THIRTY-SEVEN

March

CARI

The past week has been grueling on both Deven and I leaving us hardly any time to communicate. Myra assigned to me five time-consuming projects to be completed within five days. She must be testing me to see if I can handle it, and I will prove to her I can. Deven's schedule is nevertheless demanding between the workload of two offices, interviewing for a new assistant, and daily visits to the condo construction job site. He starts work very early in the morning and finishes very late at night leaving him with no free time. The subject of Rochelle is on hold until he returns to New York at the end of next week.

~ * ~

Rushing home after work I quickly change into my yoga gear. I grab my yoga mat and leave for class. I'm looking forward to the end of the week when Deven comes back. I miss him desperately. As I wait for the elevator, I check my Facebook page. A notification that Deven has been tagged in a photo appears. I click on the notification and a photo of Deven with his arms around two girls on each side of him pops up. One of them is his sister Kaitlin. The other is Rochelle who looks mighty cozy against him. She has her head on his shoulder, an arm around his waist, and a hand strategically placed on his washboard abs. A wave of jealousy hits me. I view the details and see that the photo was taken yesterday at the beach. When did he find time to go to the beach? My stomach turns sour and the nauseous feeling has returned.

I hurry back into the apartment. Bent over the toilet I try to throw up, but it turns out to be only a case of dry heaves. I sit on the floor with my back against the wall no longer able to feel my heart beating. I convince myself to not let the picture get to me, and force myself to go to yoga. I get there just in time and claim an unoccupied section in the corner of the room.

"Hello there." I look up and find Zach staring down at me with a gleaming smile.

"Hello, Zach."

"I haven't seen your pretty face around in a while." My cheeks redden. He's so sweet. How is he not taken?

"I've been busy."

"With your boyfriend I presume?"

Before I can answer his question, the instructor strides into the room and starts class. I had a difficult time focusing and concentrating on the techniques, and am very relieved when class is over.

"Do you have any plans tonight?"

"Not at all."

"How about I buy you a drink?"

"Um…" I look down at my attire. "I would like to change my clothes first and drop off my stuff at home."

"Why don't you change, and leave your bag in my car which is right outside? We can come back for it later."

"Great. I'll go change and meet you back here shortly."

"I'll be here waiting."

I go into the ladies locker room to change and freshen up. True to his word, he is waiting for me after he also changed. We leave our bags in his car, and walk to the bar over on the next block.

The bar is busier than usual. There is a local band performing tonight. Zach has his hand on the small of my back as we weave our way through the crowd. He sees an empty table towards the back corner and steers me to it.

"What can I get you?"

"A dirty martini please."

"Sure. Be right back with it."

I attempt to erase the picture of Deven and Rochelle out of my mind. I need a distraction, and turn my attention to the band. They are pretty awesome, but my mind wonders what Deven and Rochelle are doing right now.

"Here you go pretty lady. A dirty martini as you ordered," Zach says breaking my thoughts and handing me my drink.

I take the glass from him and take a big swallow of it.

"Are you okay there?"

Do not cry. I hold back the tears. "Yes. I'm sorry, but I don't feel so well."

"You don't look it. Do you want to go home?"

"Not yet. Let's finish our drinks first."

"Yes, of course. I'll walk back with you."

"Thanks." I take another sip of my drink.

We end up sitting through a couple of more songs and drinks before leaving the bar. I am quiet on the walk home. Zach does all the talking, and I'm grateful for his company. He walks me to my apartment.

"Will you be okay?"

I nod reassuringly.

"If there is anything you need, you know where to find me."

"Thank you Zach. And I owe you a drink."

"Nonsense. Just take care of yourself."

"I will. Good night."

"Sleep well. And good night Cari."

CHAPTER THIRTY-EIGHT

CARI

Rodrigo and Hunter decide to go on a last minute ski trip to Vermont before the ski season is over so I have the apartment to myself. Deven had planned on coming directly from the airport to the apartment, but his flight was delayed and the plane is now scheduled to arrive half past midnight. I fall asleep waiting for his text letting me know he arrived safely. I awake some time later, and reach for my phone to see what time it is. It's four in the morning, and there is a new text message on my phone.

> Cari: At last, I am home. I missed you very much and can't wait to see your beautiful face and hold you in my arms again.
> I'll come by at one. Hope you rested well.
> We have a lot of lost time to make up for.
> ILY

I turn off the phone and lay there staring up at the ceiling. I miss him and I can't wait to see him, but it doesn't change the fact that I am still hurt by the pictures of him and Rochelle.

The doorbell rings exactly at one. My heart flutters at the sight of him, and my anguish over Rochelle disappear momentarily.

"Hi," he says flashing his signature sexy dimpled smile.

"Hi." I step aside to let him in.

"I like what you did to your hair."

"Thanks."

As soon as I lock the door, he presses his chest against my back and wraps his arms around me. He smells good…woodsy, and I know he's wearing my favorite J. Malone cologne. He pushes my hair to the side exposing my neck. His lips move down my neck leaving a trail of sensual kisses. He places his hands on my shoulders and turns me around to face him. His hands move up my neck keeping them there as he lowers his head to kiss me slowly, sweetly, and tenderly. I almost let myself get swept away by his kiss when I remember the picture. I immediately pull away.

He looks baffled. "What's the matter?"

I need to get the Rochelle thing off my chest now. I move into the living room. "We have to talk," I say and sit on the couch.

He sits down beside me. "What's going on Cari?"

I let out a deep breath. "I saw a picture of you and Rochelle walking into Chateau Marmont."

He scrubs his hands down his face. Shaking his head he tells me, "It's not what it seems."

"Pray tell."

He rubs the back of his neck. "It was nothing. She was back from a shoot in Vancouver, and Kait told her I was in town so she called me. We only had dinner to catch up." She has his cell number?

"And you accepted?"

"It was only dinner."

"Why did you keep it from me that you and Rochelle were in a relationship?"

"We only went on one or two dates, but it was a long time ago. She was more of a –" He doesn't finish his sentence, but he doesn't have to. She was more of a fuck buddy to him.

I feel my lungs constricting. *Try to breathe.* "Oh God."

He slides closer to me. "She's the past Cari. She does not mean anything to me. I'm in love with you. Don't –"

The sound of the doorbell interrupts him.

"Expecting someone?"

I shake my head. "No."

Deven motions for me to stay on the couch as he goes to the door. He looks through the peephole and mumbles something incoherent.

~ * ~

DEVEN

I am just about to reassure Cari she has nothing to worry about when we hear the doorbell ring. I get up to see who is at her door. Looking through the peephole I see it's that British neighbor of hers. What the fuck does he want? I'm pleased to see the shocked look on his face when he sees me at the door. *Thought it was Cari who was going to answer didn't you arsehole?*

"Oh, hello there. I didn't know you were back. Is Cari available?" I am about to tell him to fuck off, but Cari comes to the door.

"Hi, Zach."

The arsehole is eyeing my girl, and I clench my fists.

"Hello, Cari."

"What brings you by?"

My eyes dart back and forth between them. He hands a familiar bag to Cari. Hold the fuck on. I recognize that bag. That's her yoga bag. Why does he have it?

"I wanted to return your bag to you. You left it in my car the other night, and I thought you might like to have it back for class on Monday."

She takes the bag from him. "Thanks. Would you like to come in?"

Hell no! I put my arm around her and pull her close to me. "Angel, I really missed you while I was away. You can see him at yoga and chat then."

He holds up his hands. "No, it's quite alright. I did not mean to interrupt. Thanks for the offer, but I do have to go. I just wanted to make sure you got that back."

"Thanks again Zach."

"You're very welcome. I'll catch up with you later."

"Yeah, absolutely." *Absolutely not.*

He gives me a nod which I do not return. As soon as he leaves I shut the door.

"You don't have to be so rude to him."

What? When another man is trying to take my lady away I don't have to be nice either. It's the golden rule. "Rude?"

"Yes. You were being rude when I invited him in."

"This is our time. I will not have him cut in on our time."

"I'm going to put this away," she huffs. Spinning on her heels she walks away.

I follow her to her room. Leaning on the door frame with my arms crossed I watch as she tosses the bag on her bed. I want answers now.

"Why was your bag in his car?"

"We went out for a drink after yoga the other night."

She went out with him? What the fuck? "Did I not tell you to steer clear of him?"

"He's a good person."

"Is that so? And how would you know?"

"I know because we talk. He's not a criminal." She throws her yoga clothes into her laundry basket.

"We don't know that he isn't."

She rolls her eyes at me. "He's not, and you should give him the benefit of the doubt."

"I don't trust him."

"Maybe you should try to get to know him and stop passing judgment beforehand."

"Why are you defending him?"

"I don't think you are being fair to him." She digs in her closet in search of something. I take a few steps closer to her.

"I don't want you near him especially when I am not around."

She narrows her eyes at me. "You don't want me to be around him? Well, I don't want Rochelle to be around you."

"What?"

"I know you were at the beach on Sunday with her and your sister. I saw the picture on Facebook."

Oh fuck.

"Kait begged me to go surfing with her. She refused to take no for an answer insisting I had been working non-stop and needed a break. I didn't know her bosom buddy tagged along."

"Why was Rochelle's hand on your chest?"

"It wasn't originally there. She moved her hand at the last second." I am going to have Rochelle remove that picture immediately.

"Have you no regards for my feelings?"

Oh, for Christ's sake. "Of course I have regards for your feelings. How can you think otherwise? Trust me on this please."

"Trust you? What about trusting me with Zach?"

So this is what it boils down to…trust. I trust her with Zach. It's him I don't trust.

"Zach wants you and I am blocking him from getting what he wants."

"Don't be ridiculous. He's my friend."

He's a wolf. Can't she see that? "Like Rochelle is mine."

"I don't trust Rochelle. She obviously still has the hots for you."

"She's Kait's best friend. Kait's been having some ongoing issues which I cannot divulge at this time. Rochelle has been there and continues to be there for Kait when no one else can."

"What about Ken?"

"Ken has his own shit to deal with, and he can't put up with Kait's moods."

"Why can't you tell me what the issues are with your sister?" She looks at me with imploring eyes.

"It's very complicated, and something I don't want to discuss right now."

She purses her lips, and crosses her arms. "So you'll be connected to Rochelle as long as your sister is still dealing with those issues?"

"Yes, but I swear there is nothing going on between Rochelle and I."

"Are there any more skeletons in your closet?"

Oh, there are plenty of skeletons all right, but she doesn't need to know about them because it will never affect us. "None."

She puts her hand on her forehead. "I don't think I can handle any more surprises from your past. First it was Lilah, and now it's Rochelle. What's next Deven? An illegitimate child?"

"Don't be preposterous. You kept your past about Everett from me. Tell me Cari, had he not run into you at the mall, would you have told me about him?" Let's see how she responds to that.

"That's different."

"Really? Care to tell me how it's different? We all have things in the past that we would like to keep buried."

She rubs the side of her head. "Did you sleep with Rochelle when you were in L.A.?"

What the fuck? I look at her incredulously not sure if I heard her correctly.

"What?"

"Did you sleep with Rochelle?"

It angers me that she thinks I would do something like that. "No, I did not sleep with her! I would never cheat on you. How could you even think that?" I run my hands through my long hair. "You don't have complete trust in me do you?"

She doesn't reply, but I can see it in her eyes. I don't have her full trust. I don't fucking believe this. No matter what I say she is not going to believe that I have been faithful to her. Cheating is something I do not condone. I've encountered enough of it in my life.

I can't do this if she can't trust me one hundred percent. As much as I love her, I rather let her go than be in a relationship void of trust. "The foundation of a relationship is trust. Without it, there is no relationship."

The color drains from her face. "What are you saying?" She's an intelligent girl. She can deduce what I'm trying to tell her. "Are you breaking up with me?" Her voice cracks on the last word, and it tears at my heart.

Fuck. I close my eyes, and with a heavy heart push through with it. "Maybe it's best we end this now. I don't want to be in a relationship where there is no trust."

Big, fat tears roll down her cheeks. Oh God, no. I need to get out of here. I walk out of her room, and let myself out of her apartment. As the elevator descends, I start to feel like a big douche. Did I really just end it? What have I done? Trust doesn't come easy to her. She trusted Everett and he betrayed her trust. I should go back and apologize and try to make this right. Perhaps we can work together on the trust issue. The doors open to the lobby, but I don't get off. I press the button for the fifth floor and take a ride back up.

When the doors open on her floor, I head back to her apartment, but come to a stop when I see her and her British neighbor gazing at each other. He cradles her face, wraps his arms around her, and kisses the top of her head. I boil over with anger. I wasn't even gone that long and already she's with him.

"Un-fucking-believable." The two of them turn to see me, and immediately separate. "I came back up thinking maybe we can try to work things out, but I see that was a mistake."

"No! You don't understand," she says shaking her head vehemently.

"You're wrong. It's all clear now."

"It's not what you think," Mr. Britain says. Who the fuck is speaking to him?

I don't want to hear anything either of them has to say. "You know what? I don't give a fuck anymore. She's all yours man."

I fucking gave her my heart, and in return she played me. I'm so done. I blink back threatening tears, and walk away for good.

CHAPTER THIRTY-NINE

CARI

It's been four days of agony. Four days of not being able to eat, nor sleep. Four days of crying. Four days of missing Deven terribly. And four days of trying to wrap my head around how our relationship went downhill in just a matter of minutes. Zach, Rodrigo, and Hunter take turns checking up on me, comforting me, and telling me that Deven is a fool for letting me go. Rodrigo and Hunter think it is just a misunderstanding, and insists that I continue to try to talk to Deven and explain what really happened. I sent countless texts and emails to Deven, and left plenty of voicemail messages, but all go unanswered.

I have to set Deven straight about what he thinks he saw between Zach and I. I return to work after taking a couple of days off. The first thing I do is stop by his office only to find out that he left for Los Angeles on Monday. All of my hopes vanished. His message is clear. He's done with me.

I'm determined not to shed any tears so I immerse myself into my work, and keep up a happy appearance.

"Hey. Are you feeling better?"

I glance up. "Oh, hey Alana. Um, yeah. I needed a couple of days off."

She stares at me and her eyebrows come together. "You look down. What's wrong?"

"Oh, nothing." *Keep it together Cari.*

"You're a bad liar." Alana can see right through me. "I bet you're missing Deven. Is he in a better mood? He was in such a foul mood on Monday."

Because of me. I hold back my tears, but one escapes. Darn it.

"You're not okay."

A few more tears fall. I grab a couple of tissues and wipe them away.

"Why don't we take an early lunch now and you can tell me what's wrong?"

I nod and grab my wallet out of my bag. We go to the pizzeria for lunch.

"Are you going to tell me what's going on, or am I going to have to drag it out of you?" Alana asks, and takes a bite of her pizza.

I stare down at my slice which suddenly seems unappetizing.

"Talk to me."

I look out the window watching the cars drive by, and people strolling on the street. A couple passes by holding hands looking so in love, and it reminds me of what Deven and I once had. "Deven broke up with me."

"What?"

"It's over between us."

"I'm so sorry Cari. You two seemed so happy. What happened?"

She is angry at Deven after I tell her everything.

"Trust goes both ways. He should have come clean about Rochelle, and he should have given you a chance to explain about what happened with Zach. I want to call him and straighten this out for –"

I stop her from finishing her sentence. "Please don't Alana."

"Look at how unhappy you are. How can I sit here and watch you suffer while he is being a jackass?"

I shake my head. "I will get through this." *I have to.* "I can only hope he forgives me."

"He should be the one asking for forgiveness. Don't blame yourself."

I give her a sad smile. "Thank you."

"For what?"

"For your advice, and support."

"Hey, I will always give you advice and support you. That's what friends are for."

~ * ~

During the weekend I get a surprise call from one of my college friends who is visiting New York City. Faith befriended me in one of the business courses we were taking, and was one of the very few people I hung out with besides Rodrigo during the last couple of years in college. After graduation, she remained in Boston, but we kept in touch.

It is great to reunite with Faith and catch up. I learn that she left her other job at a well-known hotel to take a higher position and salary increase at a new boutique hotel called POSH which is slated to open in about four months. She is part of the pre-opening team, and mentions there is an opening for a social media specialist. It's exactly the position I want to dip my feet in, and I ask her for more information.

When Faith gets back to Boston, I send my resume to her and she secures an online interview for me immediately. Everything after that happens quickly. A couple of days later I am offered the job. Accepting the job was easy. Telling Rodrigo, and Hunter was difficult. They pleaded with me to reconsider and apply for a similar position in Manhattan instead, but my mind was made up. I need to seize the opportunity, and make a new start somewhere far away from here where there won't be any constant reminders of Deven.

CHAPTER FORTY

April

CARI

"Any more boxes going out?" Hunter asks.

There's a box under the kitchen table, and I bend down to retrieve it. "This is the last one." I pass it to Hunter and he brings it downstairs where Zach is waiting for him. Zach is also helping me with the move.

"Looks like we have all the boxes," Alana says. Alana and her husband stopped by early this morning to help load the truck, and to see me off.

"Yeah, that's it." I scan the living room. "I'm just going to check my room once more."

I go back into my room. Opening the drawer on the night table I pull out a picture frame. I stare at the picture of Deven and I under the Rockefeller Christmas tree. It was taken the night the tree was lit. A wave of nausea suddenly hits me, and I lay down on the bed until it subsides. I didn't think seeing this picture would make me feel this way.

"You okay Cari?" Rodrigo asks.

Feeling slightly better I sit up. "Yes. I'm just feeling a little emotional."

He sits on the bed and notices that I am clutching the frame to my chest. "It's natural to feel that way, but you have to start letting him go. He hasn't even made an effort to talk to you. He doesn't deserve you sweetie."

"You're right, but it still hurts."

"But you'll get over it. New city, fresh start."

"Right. I'm going back to Boston, and leaving him behind. It's a brand new start. You won't tell him where I am if he asks you?"

"Absolutely not. I won't even bother answering his call if he even does call. I'm going to miss you like crazy."

"I'm going to miss you too." We both want to cry.

"I think we should go now before we both get all weepy."

I nod and lay the frame down on the night table. I point to the frame. "Please get rid of this after I leave."

Rodrigo nods and puts his arm around my shoulder. "It's all going to be fine. You'll start anew, and eventually you will find someone else. Someone who deserves you."

I shake my head. "No guys for a while."

"Okay. In time, you will forget about him and be ready to start dating again."

Rodrigo may be right about a log of things, but this time I think he is wrong. I may never get over Deven.

Rodrigo, Alana, Vinny, and I all go downstairs together. Hunter and Zach are waiting for us outside.

"You both take care," I say hugging Alana and Vinny.

"You too. We're going to miss you. Promise you will come back and visit often," Alana says.

"I promise, but we'll stay in touch."

"Yes, we will. Be happy in Boston." Alana's eyes are glassy. Vinny drapes his arm around her.

"I will."

"We're going to come and visit you in Boston."

"I would love that."

"We should get going Cari," Rodrigo says. I give him a nod, and walk to Zach's car.

Hunter and Rodrigo climb into the truck and drive off first. I get into Zach's car and wave to Alana and Vinny. Onto Boston we go.

CHAPTER FORTY-ONE

DEVEN

I thought leaving New York would help me forget her, but it sure as hell has not. When Brad told me that Cari had accepted a job in Boston I should have felt happy. She would no longer be at BG, or in New York. I would never run into her again, and be reminded of the fact that she played me. But I felt anything but happy.

The L.A. office is getting much busier as the company expands its west coast portfolio. My search for an Executive Assistant continues to be ongoing. No longer being able to handle the administrative work out of this office, I hire a temporary assistant. She is not great, but she will have to do for now.

I call for a meeting with my development team to go over the plans for the new constructions. Seattle, and Hong Kong are the next cities I want to start building in. I'm anticipating breaking ground in Seattle sometime over the next couple of weeks. Halfway into the meeting my temporary assistant interrupts and tells me I have an urgent phone call. I excuse myself and take the call in my office.

"This is Deven."

"Deven. It's Leigh." Her voice is trembling making the hair on the back of my neck stand. Something is wrong.

"What's wrong?"

"Dalton was just rushed to the hospital. The nurse found him unconscious. You need to come home right away."

My stomach free falls. "Yes, of course. I will book a flight and be home as soon as possible."

"Hurry back Deven. There may not be much time."

I swallow hard as I try to accept what she is saying. "I'll be there as soon as possible."

After hanging up, I waste no time and have Gwen, the temp, book a flight for me back to New York. I close my eyes and pinch the bridge of my nose remembering how lethargic he was when I last visited him a few weeks ago.

I am scared of losing my father, and angry that his life was robbed from him too soon. If only I could talk to Cari. She's the only one who understands how I'm feeling. She would tell me what I need to hear.

Fifteen minutes slipped by, and Gwen has not given anything to me yet. *Damn it.* I really need Catrina here. My patience is wearing thin with Gwen. I get up from my chair and go over to her desk.

"Have you secured a flight for me yet?"

"Hold your balls."

"Why is it taking you so long to get this done?"

"I'm still looking."

Sweet Mary, Joseph, and Jesus. She has a knack for testing my patience.

"Is every flight sold out?"

"No. Everything is expensive and there's a lot of connecting flights."

I draw in a deep breath to calm myself down before I lose it. "Cost is not an issue. I need to be on the next flight back to New York. I have a family emergency and I need to get back immediately. If you can't get this done, you will find yourself out of a job."

"Asshole," she mutters under her breath.

She is wasting time arguing with me instead of booking the flight. I think I will fly Catrina out here after all. I'll give her a raise, and get rid of nimble head.

"You have five minutes. I suggest you hurry." I turn on my heels and hear her call me a pompous ass. She is infuriating.

She comes into my office exactly five minutes later and tosses a piece of paper onto my desk. "You're booked on a three-thirty flight. Have a nice trip." So the bitch says. She's probably hoping my plane goes down mid-flight. I grab the flight itinerary and fold it up shoving it into my pocket. I grab my things and hurry back to the hotel to pack so I don't miss the flight.

~ * ~

I turn on my phone as soon as we land, and check my messages. The first text is from May. *Oh God.* Dad's gone. He passed away while I was on the flight back. I'm devastated I wasn't by his side when he died. I didn't even get a chance to say goodbye.

Everything is a blur to me as I make my way out of the airport to my car. Mauricio offers his condolences, and I thank him as he opens the door for me. I rub my eyes. I must keep it together. I have to be strong for my sister, and my mother.

Mauricio drives me to Greenwich where I will spend the night. May runs out of the house as soon as the car pulls up. I get out and pull her into my arms holding her tightly as she cries. I walk with May into the house. Mom is sitting at the kitchen table staring into space. I give her a hug. She too is putting on a strong front, but I worry about her. She just lost her husband, and though she's probably been more prepared for this moment than I have been I still worry she is going to fall apart at any minute. Our family home that has been filled with so many happy memories is now filled with nothing but sorrow.

CHAPTER FORTY-TWO

CARI

A few days after my move to Boston, Alana delivered the sad news that Dalton Blake had died. I haven't been able to stop thinking about Deven and his family, but mostly Deven. He loved his father so much.

Traffic in Connecticut is heavy on Friday night. This is the first trip I have made back to New York…a trip I didn't think I would be making so soon. Everything has been going well in Boston. I made new friends at work, and I love my new job. I even bought myself a brand new car with the money I had saved up. I don't get in until after midnight. Thank God I still have the key to let myself into the apartment. Rodrigo and Hunter have already gone to bed. I quietly take my overnight bag into my room and turn in for the night as well.

The smell of coffee wakes me up, and I pad into the kitchen to get a cup.

"Good morning gorgeous!" Rodrigo draws me in for a hug.

"Good morning," I say hugging him back.

"Hey, stop hogging her," Hunter says. Rodrigo lets me go and I hug Hunter. "How are you beautiful?" Hunter gives me a kiss on the cheek.

"I'm okay."

"You got in late last night?" Rodrigo asks.

"I got here after midnight. The traffic was backed up in Connecticut."

"Sorry we didn't wait up for you honey."

I grab a mug from the cabinet and pour coffee into it.

"How are they?" I ask as I stir the sugar in my coffee.

"Not good. Deven looked as if he hadn't slept in days; May was a

184

complete mess; and Leigh looked exhausted too."

"Deven looks like he lost weight," Hunter adds.

"I'm sure this has taken a toll on him," I reply.

"Yeah. Can't imagine it hasn't."

We finish breakfast and then prepare to leave for the funeral in Greenwich. It is insane trying to get to the church for the service. Streets are closed off, and the local police are directing traffic. We follow the detours to find additional parking, and end up parking a few streets away.

We find a pew the three of us can squeeze into inside the packed church. I recognize some people from BG, but I don't see Alana and Vinny. They're here somewhere. I text Alana to let her know we're here and where we are sitting. I can't see Deven or his family from where I am, but I hope to catch them later. The chattering ceases when the priest steps up to the altar to begin the service.

Deven approaches the altar when the priest calls upon him to give the eulogy. It is the first time I have seen him since that awful day, and he looks exactly like Rodrigo and Hunter described. There is almost a blank look to him, and it breaks my heart to see him like this. He looks down at his father's closed casket before he begins. He remains composed as he as delivers his poignant eulogy. By the time he finishes there is not a dry eye in the church.

~ * ~

DEVEN

Sleep eluded me again last night, and I ended up spending the entire night combing through pictures I had of Dad. I pulled out a few of my favorite photos of us, and placed them with him inside his casket earlier this morning.

The church is nearly filled to capacity. Dad would have been honored to know so many people came to pay their last respects. Leigh, May, and I take our seats in the front pew. Kait, Ken, Rochelle, and my biological mother sit a couple of pews behind us. I am not happy that my biological mother came to Dad's funeral, but Leigh had insisted she be allowed to attend. I wasn't going to argue with Leigh. When I look around the church again I see it is now standing room only.

At exactly ten o'clock, the service begins. The priest begins the service by reading a scripture. As the priest continues with a sermon, I pull out the index card I had prepared for the eulogy. I look over my bullet points reciting the speech in my head.

The priest calls me up to the altar. I manage to hold it together as I deliver my heartfelt tribute to Dad which is by far is one of the most difficult speeches I ever had to give. I return to my seat after I finish, and the priest continues the service with The Homily, prayers, and the communion.

As the priest prepares to conclude the church service, the pall bearers turn Dad's casket around and assume their positions alongside my father's eternal bed. The priest leads the procession out of the church. Mom, May, and I hold hands and walk behind the casket. We watch as the coffin is loaded into the hearse for its final journey. May is inconsolable. I release her hand and put my arm around her shoulder pulling her close to me. The three of us are directed to the limo behind the hearse.

We requested that only family and close friends come to the cemetery. The service is short, and after the priest says the final prayer Dad's body is slowly lowered into his final resting place. At the conclusion of the service, the mourners leave while the three of us stay behind. Mom, and May take a few steps closer to Dad's grave and silently pray before walking back to the limo. I look down at the casket and finally let the tears fall. *Good bye dad. May you rest in eternal peace.*

CHAPTER FORTY-THREE

CARI

While family and close friends are at the cemetery, the remaining mourners are invited to a buffet lunch at a local restaurant down the street and just a short walk from the church. Rodrigo, Hunter, and I meet up with Alana and Vinny at the restaurant. We find a table and sit down to chat. The moment Deven and his family arrive they are immediately surrounded. I see Mayleen heading to one of the buffet stations, and I excuse myself.

"Mayleen."

She turns around. "Oh, Cari." She immediately hugs me.

"How are you doing?"

She shrugs. "It's been so hard. I didn't want him to go yet."

"I know." And I do. I've been in her shoes. "The ache you feel will go away in time. How is your mom?"

"She's managing."

"And Deven?"

"I don't know. I think he's a mess behind the strong front he's putting on. He's been so busy with planning the funeral, and taking care of Mom and I." She puts her hand on my arm. "You should let him know you're here."

"Cari?"

I turn around to see who called my name, and there is Brad standing behind me.

"Brad!" We give each other a hug.

"I'll give you two some time to catch up. I'm going to get something to eat," Mayleen says and leaves us.

"How have you been?" Brad asks.

"Good. How about you?"

"Same here. Thanks for coming."

"I wanted to be here."

"Does Deven know you're here?" I shake my head and bite down on my lower lip.

"You should let him know you're here." Huh. Mayleen said the same thing.

Despite what happened between Deven and I, I would like to try to be friends with him. "I will, but it looks like he's constantly surrounded."

"He knows a lot of people." Brad slides his hands in his pockets. "So how is Boston?"

"Great. I think the change is good for me. And I have a car now."

"Oh, yeah? What did you get?"

"A Honda Civic."

"Instead of an Audi?"

"I can't afford that."

We spend a good time catching up before he excuses himself to talk to the other people. I begin to walk back to the table where my friends are.

"Excuse me. Carilyn Snow?"

I spin around and see a polished woman staring at me. She looks to be in her early fifties, and is dressed impeccably in a black suit with Chanel buttons.

"Yes, I am."

She gives me a once over. *Who is this lady?* "So you're the little tramp that broke my son's heart?"

My eyes grow wide in shock. Ohmigod! She must be Deven's biological mother. My anger is simmering. How dare she label me when she doesn't even know me. "Um, excuse me ma'am. I don't believe we know each other; therefore, I would appreciate if you do not label me."

She narrows her eyes resembling the evil queen in *Snow White*.

"I heard about you. You cheated on my son." Her accusation stuns me.

"I did not. You were not there. You don't know what really happened."

She points her finger at me. "I don't need to be there to know. You're just like the rest. You're after my son for his money. My son was crazy about you. And you set out to hurt him. I'm just glad he ended it with you sooner rather than later. Girls like you are nothing but trouble." Whoa! His mother is out of line.

"I can assure you ma'am that I did not set out to hurt your son."

People around us have stopped talking to watch the exchange between his biological mother and I. No longer wanting to attract attention I walk away before she attacks me again. What a total bitch!

As I make my way back to the table I see Kaitlin and Rochelle flanking Deven. Rochelle turns to him and throws her arms around his neck. His arm slides around her waist, and my stomach roils at the sight of them together. Deven does not notice me, but Kaitlin does and smirks. All of a sudden everything becomes lucid. Kaitlin is the one who misinformed her mother that I cheated on Deven. And now that I am out Deven's life her best friend can be with him. I am very angry and very hurt, and have to get out of here now.

I explain to Alana that I have to leave. Appalled by what happened she decides to leave with me. She has Vinny look for Rodrigo and Hunter and have them meet us outside. It was time to go and not turn back.

CHAPTER FORTY-FOUR

DEVEN

The amount of people who came to pay their final respects to my father was incredible. Brad's family drove from Boston to attend Dad's funeral, and that meant a lot to me. I tried to personally thank everyone for coming and as I did people shared some of their memories they had of my father and it was touching to hear their stories. Luckily, I managed to dodge my biological mother all day long.

It has been a long and exhausting day, and just about everyone has left. Mom looks extremely tired so I have Mauricio take her and May home. I stay and settle the final bill with the manager.

"You okay?" Brad asks.

"Yeah. It's over. I'm glad Dad's at peace now."

"You know he'll always be with you."

I nod. "Thanks for all of your help and support."

"You don't have to thank me. You're family to me."

I give him a man hug. I couldn't ask for a better friend.

"You ready to go?" Brad is giving me a lift back to my penthouse.

"Ready."

We walk back to the church to where his Audi A7 is parked. Brad unlocks his car and we get in. I put my seatbelt on.

"Did you get a chance to talk to Cari?"

I look over at him. "Cari was here?"

"She was. She was going to see you as soon as you were alone."

"I hardly ever had a moment alone all day." I close my eyes and lean my head back. "How is she?"

"She looks good D."

She always looks good. "Did you talk to her?"

"I did briefly."

"How is her life in Boston?"

"Good. She seems content to be back there. She even bought a car."

"Yeah?" It gives me some sort of relief that she has a car in Boston. If she is out late she does not need to rely on public transportation to get home.

"She bought a Honda Civic."

Cari does not belong in a Honda Civic. She belongs in a luxury car like a Jaguar. If we were still together I would have given her a luxury car, but we're over.

"Did she come alone?"

"No. She came with Hunter and Rodrigo."

It gives me some sort of satisfaction that she did not bring that arsehole with her to my father's funeral. "Did she mention anything about Burberry boy?"

"I didn't ask."

"Why not?"

"Because it's none of my business."

It is none of his business nor is it any of mine, but I want to know. Despite everything, I miss her so fucking much.

"You miss her." Brad has a knack for speaking my thoughts aloud.

"Fuck. Stop reading my mind."

"I can't read your mind, but I can see how miserable you have been without her. Look at you. You've lost weight, you haven't slept, and you've turned back into a super workaholic. I've never seen you like this."

I sigh. I cannot deny that he's right. "I do miss her."

"Then call her."

"No. I can't."

"Why can't you?"

Because it's over. "I just can't."

"You can't or don't want to?"

"I'm not answering the question."

Brad backs off. He knows it's not something I really want to discuss. I change the conversation to a safe subject...work.

I ask Brad to come up to the penthouse before he goes home.

"I want you to return this for me." I hand Brad the small velvet box.

He takes it and examines the box. "May I?"

"Sure." I avert my gaze. I can't bear to see the ring anymore.

He lets out a whistle. Inside the box is a three carat custom designed diamond ring I had purchased for Cari when I was in L.A. before Christmas.

"That's some rock. D, are you sure about this?"

She was everything to me. She was supposed to be my forever, and I was so ready to spend the rest of my life with her. But seeing her in the arms of another man shattered my dreams, my hopes, and my heart. Love fucking sucks.

"Yes, I'm sure. What am I going to do with it?"

He shrugs. "Hold onto it. I don't think there was or is anything going on between her and that British dude. I think you know it too. You should give her a chance to explain. I'm not convinced you are over her."

Why can't he just drop it? "Whether or not you're convinced it doesn't really matter. It's over."

"Just like that?" He's shaking his head at me. "What a shame Deven. I've never known you not to fight for something you really want."

"Don't feel like discussing this anymore. Just do me a favor and take that ring back to Harry Winston's and have them credit my account."

"Alright. I'll take care of it for you."

"Thanks man."

There's nothing but emptiness in me, and a gaping hole in my heart as the two people I love the most are gone from my life.

CHAPTER FORTY-FIVE

CARI

I was struck with a case of food poisoning after returning to Boston. Bouts of nausea and vomiting kept me home a few days, and my appetite diminished. Slowly the nausea and vomiting ease up, and my appetite returns, but I start to feel tired all the time.

Faith recommended I see her doctor, so I called and was able to get an appointment during my lunch break. I look through various magazines as I wait. After ten minutes, my name is called and I am taken into an exam room. My temperature is taken, my blood pressure checked, and as requested, I left a urine sample in a small plastic container. The doctor comes in shortly after.

Dr. Winters is a friendly and pleasant woman in her mid-fifties. She looks over my medical file and asks me what symptoms I have been experiencing. I list to her my symptoms, and her assistant returns to the room to drop off a piece of paper. The doctor looks at it and places it on the counter. She checks my lungs, ears, and throat, and then sits back down to type something into the computer.

"Carilyn, I need for you to schedule an appointment to get a sonogram done as soon as possible. We need to see how far along you are. And I am also going to recommend you to an excellent obstetrician."

Far along? Obstetrician? No. It's not possible, is it? I haven't been with anyone since Deven. And that was…oh my God.

"I'm pregnant?"

She smiles warmly at me. "Yes, Cari. You're going to have a baby."

I stare at her with my mouth agape as panic starts to set in.

To be continued…

A Note from R.C. Stern

Thank you very much for taking the time to read *FATE + CHANCE = LOVE*, the first part of Cari and Deven's story.

If you enjoyed this book, please consider leaving a review so it may be recommended to other readers. I greatly appreciate your review, and am extremely grateful for your support.

Stay tuned for the continuing story of Cari and Deven in the second installment!

Acknowledgements

To my brother: thank you for all of your support, and for always being there for me. I'm truly lucky to have such a fabulous brother. You are absolutely the best.

To my friends who have been with me when I first set out to do this a while back: many, many thanks to each of you for the support you have given to me.

To my dear friend who has been on this journey with me from the start: thank you for your constant encouragement and support to get this done. You are truly an amazing friend, and I am blessed to have you in my life.

To my two musketeers: thank you for listening, for cheering me on, and for keeping me sane. I am so thankful to have you both in my life.

To my friend that always has my back: thank you for believing I could do this.

To "DAH": I still recall when I first told you that I wanted to do this. You have had so much faith in me every step of the way, and I can't express how much that has meant to me. Thank you so much.

To Daniela at Stunning Book Covers: thank you very much for creating such a gorgeous cover. It's a pleasure to work with you.

And finally, to my family who have had to put up with me while I juggled writing, work, home, and everything else in between: thank you, thank you, thank you for all the love and support you have given me. Love you all. XOXOXO

Connect with R.C. Stern

http://www.facebook.com/authorrcstern
http://www.twitter.com/author_rcstern